SARAH
JANE

Books by James Sallis

SARAH JANE

JANE

JAMES

SALLIS

Published by
Soho Press, Inc.
227 W 17th Street
New York, NY 10011

Library of Congress Cataloging-in-Publication Data

Sallis, James, 1944– author.
Sarah Jane / James Sallis.

ISBN 978-1-64129-080-7
eISBN 978-1-64129-081-4

1. Mystery fiction.
PS3569.A462 S27 2019 I DDC 813'.54—dc23

Interior design by Janine Agro

Printed in the United States of America

10 9 8 7 6 5 4 3 2 1

To my students,
who help me remember
why this is so important

... from that day forward she lived
happily ever after. Except for the dying
at the end. And the heartbreak in between.

—Lucius Shepard

Memory is a hunting horn
It dies along the wind

—Apollinaire

1.

My name is Pretty, but I'm not. Haven't been, won't be. And that's not really my name, either, just what Daddy calls me. Beauty's only skin deep, he used to say, so when I was six I scratched my arm open looking for it. Scar's still there. And I guess it's like everyone saying if you dig deep enough you'll find China. All I got from that was blisters.

My real name is Sarah Jane Pullman. Kids at school call me Squeaky. At church I'm mostly S.J. or (as Daddy's girl, a real yuck for the old guys in their shiny-butt suits standing by the Sunday School door having a cigarette) I'm Junior. Seems like everyone I know calls me something different.

I wrote all the above in a diary when I was seven. It wasn't a real diary, it was a spiral-bound notebook, the kind you got for school, with a daisy-yellow cover that said *Southern Paper* and wide-spaced lines. For security I kept a paperclip on the pages in a changing pattern, how many pages got clipped together, where on the page. Who

I thought might want to sneak in and read what a seven-year-old wrote about her life, I can't now imagine.

Back then we were raising chickens, six thousand of them at a time in long buildings like army barracks, this the most recent of money-making gambits that included selling dirt from the hills behind the house, building backyard barbeque pits for people, and doing lawn-mower repair. We'd pull sweet little chirpy chicks out of corrugated boxes, then months later wade in among terrified chickens, snag them by their legs, and cram them into cages to get stacked on trucks and hauled away. You had to move fast or they'd pile up in corners of the houses and smother.

Not that my parents were lacking. They worked their butts off, holding down regular jobs then coming home to this. Loading and unloading fifty-pound sacks of food, turning the sawdust litter daily, scooping and replacing it on schedule, making sure there was water and that the gas heaters in the brooders were good, jets clear, gas low and steady, no leaks. But there wasn't much money to be had in the town and what money there was, most of it flowed from and went back, having grown like the chicks, to the Howes or the Sandersons.

I grew up in a town called Selmer, down where Tennessee and Alabama get together and kind of become their own place, in a house that spent the first sixteen years of my life getting ready to slide down the hill, which it did right after I left. Daddy moved into a trailer then and never much left it so as you'd notice. I don't want to say much about my marriage to Bullhead years later and all that. More scars.

But I didn't do all those things they say I did. Well, not all of them anyway.

Mom wasn't around much after I got to be ten. Nobody talked about it. She'd be gone, for weeks, months, then one morning walk out of the big bedroom and be around a while, moving here to there in the house like a stray piece of furniture we were trying to find a place for.

Once she left in the middle of a movie, didn't say a thing, just walked away, some stupid comedy about a couple who had a first date and kept not being able to get together for a second one because of weather and cute animals and traffic jams and parades. My brother and I watched the rest of it, right up to the big ending with the guy stage right and her stage left and big open spaces between. Darn and I waited outside for half an hour before begging a city bus driver to let us ride home free, since we didn't have any money. My brother's name was Darnell, but everyone called him Darn.

Daddy looked up from mixing a milk punch at the kitchen counter when we came in. "Huh. Gone again," he said.

I told him she'd be back.

"I expect she will." He took a sip, added more sugar. "Life's not the pizza place, Pretty. It don't deliver."

———

We're speeding along at 23 mph in that all-forsaken foreign desert and there's dust over to the right. East or west, who knows. There's not much by way of landmarks out there, you have to look at the compass. Damned sun's everywhere, so that's no help either. Oscar pulls the jeep over to get some idea how far away the dust is, what direction the vehicle's moving, how fast. Our engine's idling, but the bucks and jolts and bottom-outs are stamped into our bodies. We still feel them. Oscar doesn't have sweat stains under his arms and I'm thinking Damn, this man's not human, he's some kind of alien. Some creature.

You ever think about having kids, Oscar asks me. Weird shit comes up out there in that deadly sunlight, conversations you'd never have anywhere else. Like the featurelessness around you draws it out. Someday I mean, he says.

I don't tell him I already had one.

Six hours after I had her, two or three in the morning, they told me they'd done all they could but my baby had died. They brought her for me to hold, wrapped in a pink blanket. Her face was ghostly white. Had she ever really lived? An hour after they left, I was gone.

Nope, I told Oscar.

The shadow of a bird comes across us as it flies above. We watch the shadow move away from us, toward a distant dust devil. The engine pings. Smells hot. Everything smells hot.

Just the way weird shit comes up out there, words can start to get away from you. Sentences won't hang together, they have holes in them. Verbs drop out, answers don't fit questions. With losses like that, you have to wonder if what we think, what we're *able* to think, gets dialed down too.

Moving away from us, Oscar says. One vehicle, you think?

Looks like.

And we're moving again.

Oscar with less than an hour left to live.

A year after I left Selmer, on my seventeenth birthday, I was on a bus nosing slowly northward always within sight of the river, like a boat gone off course and sniffing out some access that had to be just ahead. The family behind me, parents, two kids maybe eight and six, bought box lunches when a vendor came aboard at a rest stop. Fried chicken, biscuits the size of saucers, cole slaw. Familiar food for the long, uncertain voyage to somewhere else. All four had serious body odor; oil sparkled in the man's and the boy's hair. Even then I knew this signaled something. I found out what, when the boy walked to the front of the bus and came down row by row, repeating the same phrase, a Slavic language of some sort, I think, at each. Foreigners. So much for familiar food. They were embarked on an adventure as brave and as foolhardy as my own.

I came to ground somewhere past St. Louis, in a college town whose population halved whenever school let out, flatland unrolling to every side, geographically so ambiguous that you couldn't tell if you were still in the South or had tumbled ass-end-up into some not-Kansas. Place had once been a farmhouse, in times long past had got sectioned up for student rentals, then in its slow, sure decline endured torn-out walls till all that remained were two arenas, one for those in bed or sleeping, one for those not. A stream of passers-through came and went about a core of regulars. Gregory called the temporaries *mayflies*. Some days he was himself a fly, as in fly-in-the-ointment, other days he was our mentor, leader, truthsayer, shaman. He *knew* shit, right? For sure he did.

We met at the student union where I hung around awaiting the great or small whatever. I figured with that many young people, so many hundreds of in-between lives, stuff had to be happening. Moments would crackle, shadows jump like crickets. Gregory found me in the cafeteria lurking over my second hour-long cup of coffee in the still, blanched afternoon of my fourth day. He took me home, gave me a bologna sandwich and bedded me, threw me back in the water.

I swam.

"Here's what it comes down to," Gregory said, "wandering to find direction. All of it. The more you wander, the more direction you find." Rain scattered like birdshot on the roof, rolled hopefully into gutters packed with years of detritus, gave up and bailed. About us we could hear breathing, sighs and farts, whispers of dream-time conversations.

"There were these guys that used to play in the next building over. Years ago, when I was older than you but not by much. And I'd listen. The drummer'd play three beats, drop out for maybe six, come back in for one, the bass thumped away irrespective of tonal center or time signature or any need to *keep* time, the guitarist's hand never once strayed from the tremolo bar, milking it, stretching a single note like an elastic band about to pop over nine, ten almost-measures. What the hell *was* that? So I kept listening. And after a while I found my way in. It was a music of pure potential, music that never quite came into being, that refused to surrender a single possibility."

Deep.

Not that he didn't have hold of something.

Gregory had hold of a lot of things. Some of it real, much of it not. He threw out lines like someone fishing close to shore from a boat. Meanwhile, all kinds of stories about him banged up against one another. He'd killed a woman up in Canada, or almost did, or she'd tried to kill him. He'd been a professor at Antioch and one day walked away from it. He was on the run from government agents. He'd lived in a commune near Portland which he left weeks before an FBI raid. What the stories had in common is that in all of them he fled.

Everybody called the place Cracker Barn, and it didn't take long before I had my Cracker Barn best friend. I'd gone to grab some sleep, this was my third or fourth day there, only to find all the mattresses occupied. On one of them near the door a skinny girl with too much eye makeup raised her head like a turtle, body not moving at all, just the head poking up, scooched over and patted the ticking next to her. Why the hell not. She probably wasn't already talking when I woke up hours later, but it seemed that way. She hailed from Scottsdale, Arizona, "where people live right. But I never could make sense of the rule book. Hell, they wouldn't even give me a copy of the fucking rule book. Like I was supposed to just *know*."

What *I* knew about Arizona came down to cactus and cowboys and hot, which years later turned out to be pretty much it.

Shawna had been at the Barn a long time. The year before, Gregory bought a cake for her twenty-first birthday and they had a party. I found out about that when I asked wasn't someone looking for her and she said they'd have given up by now. She'd been my age, seventeen, when she left. Told me how she stood at a bus station on 16th Street in Phoenix looking at destinations painted on the side wall, Albuquerque misspelled, whited out for repainting or mostly, then misspelled again.

It was at the Barn that I first felt a life taking shape around me. I learned to cook there, chiefly from self defense since no one else was up for it and what came to the table was often unrecognizable and always horrible. Took some doing to get the hang of it, but I had a resident supply of experimental subjects. Cooking proved to be a skill that put me in good stead, as books say, in later life. I also started to learn to read body language there, figuring out how to look behind what others said and what they thought they were saying, all the shady stuff lurking back there.

Sometimes, especially late at night, Gregory's stories tumbled over the cliff into true weirdness, like when he started talking about how he invented underclothes.

"We were just sitting around one day, my friend Hogg and me, in the kitchen as usual with a bottle of something, drinking the heart out of a fine summer afternoon, and it came to me. I sketched them out on the table with a flat carpenter's pencil. That was a long time ago, a few weeks after we came up with mushrooms, tubas and wasps, or maybe right before. Never thought for a minute the damn things would catch on. Never once saw a penny from any of it."

We can't ever know how others see the world, can't know what may be rattling around in their heads: loose change, grand ideas, resentments, pennies from the fountain, spiffed-up memories, codes and ciphers.

That knowledge was the most important thing I carried away from Cracker Barn.

"Had you awareness of your peers' intent, Miss Pullman?"

No downtown *Did you have* for this refined lawyer lady with her tailored suit and silk scarf artfully draped. Maybe if I stared real, real hard, the scarf would start to tighten, strangle her slowly. She'd reach up and touch it. Touch it again, harder. Stagger a step or two. Eyes begin to bulge.

And *peers* rather than *friends* or *crew*—another quality touch.

Since I'd left the Cracker Barn, some weird stuff had gone down, weirder still awaiting me, stuff I couldn't then imagine, just ahead.

Judge Fusco didn't allow water in his courtroom, they said, because it slowed things down. I sure could have used some.

He had no problem allowing fans, though. They were everywhere. Three overhead, circling sluglike to drag shadows across the ceiling, a table oscillator on the bench beside him. Close by, a box fan tilted to bounce off the back wall like a rock band's amplifier.

Had I awareness, like she asked? Well, awareness comes in all shapes and sizes, doesn't it? Knowledge too. But yeah, at some level I must have known. Usually we do.

I started trying to say that and the lawyer stopped me.

"Yes or no, Miss Pullman?"

I opened my mouth again and Yes came out.

My court-appointed lawyer looked all of sixteen, had hair like pubes, his second chin a stand-in for the other's scarf, and he did what he could. But from that point it was a slam dunk, right up to Judge Fusco telling me to rise and saying that while some would question his decision, he was old school, and in light of my youth (of which there had not been all that much, light I mean) and my obvious contrition (really?) he was giving me a choice: go to jail, or join the armed services.

I saluted the old fart, right then and there.

As a child I'd lie in bed at night, in absolute dark out on town's edge where we lived, wrapped in a dull thrum from the generator sub-station atop Crow's Ridge nearby, and try to imagine not being, to envision a world without me. My mind groped forward, small steps at first, then bolder, ever reaching. I'd wake with no idea where I was, with no sense of self, my mind floating free. And when the world in time began to right itself, every connection between mind and body was lost. My arm refused to rise into the darkness before me. My legs wouldn't move however forcefully I summoned them. In that pitch black there were only sounds: the hammer of my heartbeat, the thrum from Crow's Ridge, the wordless hum of the radio from my father's bedroom. The world's static.

———

Another thing Daddy did, along with raising chickens, selling off dirt and building brick barbeque pits, was he got called on to fix things from time to time.

Like Jenny Siler's problem with the King boys. They were two strong, Daniel and Matthew, Bible names, and their father had disappeared when they were kids, buried somewhere in the swamp, everybody said, which served him right as the man had been born no good, and the list a long one as to who might have put him to rest there. Daddy was of the opinion that the boys had been looking for something, maybe for their old man without knowing it, ever since. They did their looking mostly on other people's property, in other people's houses, among other people's possessions.

First, small things started to go missing at Miss Siler's. Pearl earrings and an insect brooch with jewels that looked real for eyes, her long-dead brother's silver baby spoon, an engagement ring she wore for six weeks when she was thirty-four. Saturday last, she came out on the back porch and found her dog Simon halfway up the stairs, stiff and cold, tongue swollen out of his mouth. Poisoned. Old Simon had been hit by cars and trucks twice, shot by hunters, lost a leg, and survived it all. Now look at him. When Miss Siler came by with an apple pie baked in a pan that could have been a Civil War relic, Daddy listened to her, nodded, and said he'd see to it.

Why don't you just call the police? I asked him. In school this was what they said we were supposed to do.

We're from good hillbilly stock, Pretty. We don't call police.

Daddy paid the boys a visit. Next day they were gone, never to be seen again in these parts. Daddy said he reckoned they might have finally found their worthless old man.

First you smell the target material. Pulverized stone, cement. Hot metal. Then the reek of the explosive itself comes up under in waves. Ammonia, chlorine. A hard sting to it. Gets in your nose and can't be dislodged.

We'd been sitting watching the dust devil, trying for a fix on how many and how far. I remember Oscar dropping it in gear and pulling away again. I look over and his mouth is open and there's no sound. Then I'm on the ground looking sideways at the jeep trying to right things in my head, figure out which of us is upside down, and Oscar's pulling himself toward me from what looks like half a mile away, barely moving, and when my head clears I see why. He's holding his leg on with one hand, pulling himself along with the other. Not much left of the leg.

My legs don't want to work either, but I can crawl, so I do that and get to him. Just like before, his mouth is moving and I don't hear anything. Then I realize that I don't hear anything at all, just this roar in my ears.

The leg's completely gone below the knee, the rest connected only by flaps of skin. I'm thinking how it looks like fringe on old fake-buckskin jackets and holding his hand when he stiffens, blinks, and stops breathing.

Had to be an RPG. So where are they? Why would they fire and not come on in?

Strange how much of your world goes away when you can't hear. I had a nose full of bleach and nothing in my ears but ocean.

But when you're down, in the absence of active fire you stay down. Wait it out. Assess. That had been drilled into me.

Lots more bleach and ocean and smoke, then I felt vibrations from the ground behind me. Footfalls. Very close. A foot poked at me, moments later pushed under and kicked up, withdrew. I was breathing as shallowly as possible. Three toes of a bare foot showed at the edge of my vision. Stopped there. Kicked at my head. I could no longer see the foot then, but shortly felt whoever it was tugging hard at my boot. Down there, probably kneeling, trying to get the boot off.

I had to take this chance, along with the chance that there was only the one of them. Sheath knife in hand, I did the quickest sit-up of my life and thrust—blindly, by feel, where I thought he would be. He was small. And sitting, not kneeling. The knife struck him squarely in the throat. Driven by air bursting from a ruptured trachea, blood spray covered me. His face never once changed. His hands were still on my boot as he fell.

He may have been all of twelve or thirteen.

He could be fodder, of course. In the cities they recruited them that young and younger. But it was just as possible that he'd simply come upon an abandoned weapon and taken it. I waited some more and when no one else showed up, I embraced the latter.

Most of a full day went by, they tell me. All of it for me a bleed, a blur: dark leeching out from the bright center, zigzags of blindness, flashes, flares, empty spaces. Firmly believed myself to be heading back to the compound, keeping the sun to my left, but the sun kept moving, the sun was everywhere, right, left, full ahead, behind.

Another patrol came across me by accident. I asked if they were here to take me home. When they asked where's home, I couldn't remember. We had chickens, I told them.

Memory of the site, of where we'd been, was gone. I relayed what I could, and a team went back out to where they picked me up. Eventually they found the vehicle, but both bodies were gone. Oscar's tags turned up in my pocket. I had no memory of taking them.

2.

Close to a year later, not long before I met up with Bull-head, I'm cooking in this resort that's fitted out like a hunting lodge, with dark beams where no beams had gone before and walls of untreated wood that make it look like splinters are hanging off but even the splinters are sheathed in clear varnish. It's mid-July, so hot the sweat lifts off you before you know it's there. College boy Erik the Red has placed a breakfast order so vast that I have to look out to see if this could really be for a single person. The man's sitting at the corner table in Erik's station, alone all right, thumping at the glass to attract the attention of a squirrel outside among the shrubs, mostly sage and rosemary. Suit coat's too big, regulation white shirt, ambiguously blue tie with some pattern I can't make out from here. Last time he saw a barber was during cold weather. Something that looks like the love child of a lunchbox and a plastic briefcase in the chair beside him.

Man might weigh a hundred-and-ten soaking wet and he's ordered enough food for three.

I go back through the kitchen doors, throw eggs in the blender for the omelet, grab pancake batter from the cooler, check on the bacon bin to be sure it's well stocked. 'Ski looks over to tell me he's got to leave early today for an appointment with the immigration service. 'Ski's Russian, came in as a student, now his visa's expired and he's angling to stay. "Why're you telling me?" I ask. "Go tell Lizard." Day-shift manager, Tony Lasardo. "I'm telling you because you're the only one who gives a shit," 'Ski says. Man should get immigration points for nailing American vernacular.

Two P.M., after lunch rush, my shift's done, and I decide to swing by the arts and crafts festival downtown near the college. They close off the streets and let them fill with booths of jewelry, paintings, tie-dye clothing, lawn sculptures, blown glass and ceramics, boutique soap and dehydrated soup, chocolate-covered frozen bananas, kitsch and tchotchke of every sort. The streets fill with people too—though, hot as it is, along with the stands of port-a-potties there ought to be hose-down stations.

Squint hard, you can imagine you're back in the bazaars that were everywhere over in sandworld. Different languages and different smells but the same bustle, same clogs and clots of people, same *too much*.

Something always follows me home. Soap dish shaped like a bear paw, wall hangers in the form of beckoning fingers, a tiny ceramic wombat. Once in a great while, an item goes immediately into use. Most remain where they touch ground, on table tops, shelves and random surfaces. A few lead immigrant lives, migrating from place to place until at length they fade into the general population.

Speaking of which, population, today at the festival it consists of young women about to fall off the front of their canted shoes, well-groomed guys in plaid shorts and expensive leather slip-ons without socks, prides of fiftyish women in flowery blouses and perfect hair with a million urgent things to say to one another, couples strolling behind trophy dogs, children of every age swarming as though chum has been scattered.

Flip-flops slap out rhythms, voices rise and fall, there's the scent of perfumes and colognes, grilled meat, burned sugar, hot pavement and sweat, as moments sink into memory vaults of minds and cameras.

Afterward I stop at one of many trendy shops for over-priced coffee, so I'm late getting home, which just now is a one-room apartment elevated to something grander, in the ad if not in fact, by virtue of being a separate building. The house it once stood behind in order to serve as storage, workshop or secondary residence is gone. A pool of crisply browned grass and weeds stretches wanly toward the street.

Rarely hungry after ten hours of smelling food and breathing fire, I put my new spoon rest in the sink where someday soap and water will happen upon it, grab the apple with the fewest brown spots from the bowl, and make for the great outdoors, into my favorite time of day, darkness closing shell-like from above and below.

Often when I'm out of an evening walking, I look into windows as I pass and catch glimpses of shows on TVs inside. What I see there is wildly unrelated, fragments of movies, of sitcoms and detective series, reruns of *Get Smart*, nature and history documentaries, that nonetheless get strung together in my mind as I shuttle between windows, the amalgam ever so much more interesting than what's actually taking place in those TVs and living rooms.

Tonight's show could be about a paralyzed man, a veteran, who works as a sit-down comic at the hippest bar in town, solving mysteries in his spare time while raising a rare species of bird that will save the world from giant tomato worms by singing to them. In between, he thinks and squints a lot.

Another thing I do out walking is watch the gait and carriage of fellow pedestrians. The fascination with body language that I picked up back at the Cracker Barn, for what people signal beneath the facades they present, persists. This twentyish man in cargo shorts and knock-off cross trainers, for instance, whose head seems to move independently of his body. Or how a young woman wearing a plain summer dress brings her right foot around in a slight arc. The elderly gentleman replacing his self-dialogue with a bright smile, as though a switch has been thrown, as we approach one another.

Stories there. Lives. Worlds.

Back home (I always feel the word *home* should be indicated by quotation marks, italics, extra spaces for breath) I grind a couple handfuls of Blue Mountain, pour hot water into the French press and, when the time comes, push on the plunger as though I've just shouted *Fire in the hole*.

The coffee's dark, deeply rich and layered, mysterious. "Smells like good dirt, like newly turned earth," my friend Vickie (née Victor) used to say, "and tastes like it's left Earth behind for a better place." Vickie never for a moment believed there *was* a better place, but that sounded dead on.

I read as I drink my coffee, do fifty pushups, and eat two apples. The pushups stayed with me from basic and from weeks of hanging out with nothing to do in-country. Apples were kind of what I lived on back then. I'd once heard a musician explaining how he survived on the road. Eat a lumberjack's breakfast and nothing but a bunch of apples the rest of the day, he said.

The days march by and extraordinary things happen all around us. Small miracles, haphazard events, bursts of joy, revelations. An old man painfully gets to his knees to stroke the dying cat he found on his patio. A shy child hears live music for the first time and dances. Thousands of fireflies in the Smoky Mountains blink their tail lights every one at the same time. We hunker down in our daily lives, in the shelter of routines and assumptions. We miss so much.

———

"I carry my country inside myself, I *am* my country. Like in the song: *This world has never been my home.*"

I was cooking in a diner some five hundred miles, three months, and seven change-of-plans from the resort, Eric the Red, and squirrels. He came in one night out of nowhere with his entourage, posse, peeps, homies, minions, take your pick, your pick being dependent on when you were born, where you grew up, your politics, disposition, a slew or a mess of other things. Frankly, not one of the troop lined up with him looked as though he or she belonged any damned where.

But there they were at the door, backlit by streetlights, posing for a moment (or so it seemed) before coming in.

Some kind of actor, I knew that much from the general chatter. A painter turned performance artist, as it turned out. And that night he rode, a sidekick told me, the horse of silence, communicating in a made-up sign language somehow as beautiful as it was dorky. "Horse, huh?" I said. "Then I'll have to be careful where I step." "Hey, the hell with silence," the horse's rider said.

It was a week or so later he said that about carrying his country around. We were in my crappy, cagelike apartment getting ready to go out and leave the roaches, mice and mosquitoes to their respective tasks, and we'd been talking, not a clue how that would ever come up between us as a topic of conversation, politics. He said he had none.

"That's not possible," I said.

He knew as little about my past as I knew of his. Nothing at all about the so-called service to my country for which soldiers were always getting thanked in TV shows and movies.

"You have to have some sense of what's right," I went on, "of what needs to be worked for, fought for."

"In the world I see, working for things doesn't make much difference. How things are, that gets sneaked in from below when you're not looking. Or it just fucking crashes down from five stories up."

Grim, and not much room for gray. But in truth, at the time not a far cry from the world I saw too.

He pulled on a work boot, one of those weird yellow-orange lumps from Target and dollar stores. "Groucho Marx said he wasn't crazy about reality but it's still the only place to get a decent meal."

That's when he told me about being his own country and not of this world.

For some time I avoided attending Olin's performances ("Born Colin, never liked that damn C, so I let it go"), figuring with what went on back home and with my stay in the desert I'd had more than my fill of weird. When I finally relented and sat through one, nothing came up that wasn't familiar from the day-to-day. Sign language. The elaborately smiling face above a body weighed down by sadness. A soundless tuba player with puffing cheeks.

Lengthy free-associative talks about what the moon did on its weekends or how Who and Whynot shoulda been bigger stars. The sorrowful angel who comes to earth to save us and turns imperceptibly, so slowly and subtly that you don't realize until it has happened, into a devil.

Servers knew him as a regular. Olin was vegetarian ("One of my few virtues, or perhaps simply pretension") and the diner's owner was Greek, with hummus and tabouli always at hand. A match. Vegetarians being about as common as Beemers in our part of town, my fellow workers found the practice mystifying.

Three months after Olin and I met, the owner died, and with no one in the family interested in taking the helm, Silver's went up for sale. Some guy from uptown arrived with a gaggle of fleshly echoes tiptoeing in his wake. Words like gentrification and going upscale didn't get said aloud, but they were there, tugged above the crew like cartoon thought balloons. I took one look, took a walk, went looking.

Fats at Step Up told me he made a great soup. The shelter opened every evening at six and served a meal. Fats was rail thin. Everyone called me Curly, he told me, till my hair fell out. Hard to be sure whether or not he meant that as a joke.

"I make a great soup," he said again. "Oh, and corn-meal muffins every other night."

"That's it?"

"They like us to keep it simple."

Ah, *they*.

So we went on keeping it simple, Fats and me, but simple with a difference. Kept the soup, added biscuits and the occasional fruit salad, even red beans and rice.

Step Up was the fourth job I interviewed for after walking out of the diner. The first was line cook at a semi-swank midtown restaurant, get there at 2 P.M. and stay till midnight dripping sweat onto the grill and stovetop with people yelling at you as you did what you could to resuscitate dodgy fish and prefab sauces. I'd never in my life been desperate enough. After that, I answered a blind ad that turned out to be a school cafeteria of the sloppy joes on Tuesday, fish sticks on Friday persuasion. The third, another cafeteria of quite a different sort, might have been interesting. It was in the home office of a vast alternate-energy corporation, employees only, two hundred or more of them. But the HR guy who caught the interview somehow also caught on to the military background I'd left off my résumé, fellow grunt and all that, where'd you see action, and that was a weight I didn't want to carry.

Then the shelter. Step Up.

Felt like home when I stepped through the door.

Sometimes Olin would come down to help serve, or to do whatever was needed, he said, but often as not he'd wind up sitting with our patrons, listening to their stories and spinning his own. Keeping his chops up, as he put it.

What Olin said about himself, you could never tell how much was true, how much dressed up for Sunday. And the people clustered around him like lumps in oatmeal—producers, a short-lived agent or two, other performers, musicians, hangers-on—changed with the seasons. I suppose some were friends, but I could never sort them. Here and there I did garner bits and pieces that seemed real, scraps really, of Olin's life, like the time he fell off a mountain while hiking. How did it change him, someone asked, had it changed the way he lived. Yeah, I keep low to the ground now, he said.

Olin's own frequent comment regarding the fall and much else was "I'm the man with no more past," after which he'd frown till his eyebrows dipped toward his nose, perform a Gallic-style shrug, and add: "Some old Frenchman."

When he disappeared, left me in the park waiting for him as afternoon wore into evening, I really wasn't all that surprised. I bought bagged popcorn at a nearby convenience store and sat feeding it to pigeons. There got to be fewer and fewer of them, then none, and streetlights came on. Five weeks later I got a postcard with a bathing beauty playing a banjo on the front.

> *In Georgia. Crazy beautiful here. Miss you.*
> *Colin. P.S. I started using the C again.*

3.

The police were at the door. And I was sound asleep in someone's left-behind T-shirt and a pair of panties that had started out pink back about the time of our last recession. That, and hungover from godawful wine out of industrial-size jugs.

Even the cop in front, and these guys see everything, hit pause when I opened the door. His eyes went from my troll-doll hair to the *d EAD b EAT* logo on the shirt before getting pulled back up, by force of will, to my face.

As for me, I'd apparently left behind all my words at last night's roost, and just leaned against the door frame. Didn't need words. Didn't need clothes. Greet visitors in baggy underpants and a see-through T-shirt. How I lived now.

"Morning, ma'am," the cop said, "Sergeant Barnes," as I got a glimpse of his badge and first name *Charles* on the ID. "Okay if we come in?"

I moved out of their way. Sergeant Barnes was as under-spoken in appearance as in speech, with plain, blunt features and a practiced smile, a senior salesman at Best Buy sort. His partner came across as more the athletic type, wide shoulders, legs apart, low center of gravity. That one didn't identify himself but handed me his cup of Starbuck's, saying he hadn't drunk from it yet and it looked like I needed it more than he did.

From next door came the sound of raised voices, Susie and Bud's regular go-to. Most of the time it stayed verbal.

The coffee donor looked that way.

Stop fucking with me, Suze.

"Sorry," I said. "Thin walls. Never get too lonely round here."

There's that tongue of yours again. Oughta keep that thing in a jar.

"This happen often?" Officer Coffee asked.

Along with your cunt! Keep it home that way!

"What do you think?"

"It ever go stronger?"

"Sometimes, yeah, it does."

"Back in five, Charlie," he said, and left.

Sergeant Barnes shook his head, smiling his smile. "Man can't help himself. In his own mind he's . . ." He stopped and looked down at the floor a moment. Meant to indicate sincerity, I'm pretty sure.

"In *my* mind I'm still in bed sound asleep."

"Sorry about that . . . Have you lived here long, Miss Pullman?"

"Why?"

He shook his head again the same way he had for his partner. "What I'm wondering is how well you know your neighbors."

"Next door, you mean."

"Or down the hall—Daniel Eskew?" Even with the uptilt at the end it didn't sound like a question.

Officer Coffee came back, said he'd had a little talk with Mr. Oliver over there, let him know he'd be looking in from time to time.

"Main thing we need to know is when you last saw Daniel Eskew," Barnes said.

I tried to remember as I sipped the coffee. No milk, no froth, no subversive flavoring. Not bad, really. Black and strong.

"Today's what?"

"Thursday."

"Monday, then. Dinner, drinks, dalliance."

"Dalliance." That from the newly returned hero.

"They still make it."

"Like whoopie, huh."

"Never out of style."

"Do you know where he might be reached?" Barnes said, interrupting our comedy fest. "A work address, maybe?"

I had to laugh. "Work's a four-letter word in a language he doesn't speak."

"Nothing for us, then?"

"Sorry."

"*You're* employed, right, Miss Pullman? As a chef."

"Cook. Night shift, when misfits have the restaurant and pretty much the rest of the city to themselves. An uncomplicated life."

Barnes did the floor thing again. "What we all long for."

"And so few have the good sense and good luck to find."

"If an uncomplicated life's what you're after," his partner said, "you want to reconsider consorting with the like of Dan Eskew."

"Consorting, huh?"

"Or Dom Larson—one of his other names."

"Any chance I could get back to sleep while I'm reconsidering?"

"Absolutely," Sergeant Barnes said. "Thank you for your time."

I held up the Starbuck's. "Thanks for the coffee."

"Nothing to it. Saw someone in need."

"The police are your friends?"

"They can be."

"Sometimes," Sergeant Barnes said.

You never know what's floating down toward you as you plod your way upstream.

"He had been in Mobile, like you said—old news. After

a while we picked up the trail in New Orleans. Metairie, really. Across the river. But by then he'd gone ghost again."

We were sharing buffalo wings at SleazEazy's, a neighborhood bar B.H. favored. Last time I saw him, he'd given me his coffee. Now he was buying me a meal. This was other people's neighborhood, not his, not mine. He'd come across it while on a case, looking for "a piece of dirt about to come to the worst end," and fell for the place, had been dropping in routinely ever since. He had his jacket off in the ninety-degree weather, holster and gun stark against the well-pressed, wilting white dress shirt. Above us, a fan with unequal blades circled, dipped, wobbled back upright.

"You know I don't give half a damn, right?" I said, licking fingers. By my bright orange cuticles you shall know me.

Scary how selective our memories can be. Did I simply rationalize what had taken place on his and his partner's visit, file it away in some recess of my mind? Decide that what I heard next door, the single declarative sentence followed by a collision that shook the walls of my apartment, had to be other than what it was? Somehow I had contrived to misremember, disremember, ignore. In subsequent months I'd hone that skill to a fine, keen edge. Me, so confident in my ability to peel back appearances and get true reads on people.

"We understood that you were close."

"More like convenient."

A slight pause, like a hitch in the step or a hiccup. "I see."

"Standing in as moral watchdog *and* protector?"

"Haven't had much luck at either. Trying to get to know you is all. And provide a word of caution. We have reason to believe the man you know as Dan Eskew may be heading back this way."

"No worry. Not exactly convenient anymore, is he?"

"Just be aware. And should he try to contact you—"

"He won't."

"—give us a call."

"And here I thought you were courting me for my quick wit and silky, smooth body."

"Courting."

"As in courtly love?"

"Per Gaston Paris, 1880 or so."

"For that you need a high-born woman."

"One works with what one has."

"Or what one doesn't . . . So, I guess cops go to college these days."

"Some like 'em smart."

He went to the bar to grab a couple more beers and lingered a while talking with a stocky middle-aged man sitting there. Cloth slouch cap, dark blue windbreaker, khakis, work boots. Had one of those faces that look to have been compacted, like some heaviness had weighed it down and pushed out the sides.

"Sorry," he said when he came back. "Jimmy Gunter.

Bought up land near downtown when it was cheap, built a chain of warehouses and storage facilities, retired at forty."

"Old friends?"

"Went to school with my brother. But he gets around, knows everyone, either side of the fence."

We sat quietly, watching people come and go. The bartender's left arm was about half the length of the right and seemed to have no elbow. Didn't slow him down at all.

B.H. had come round "to follow up" a week or so after he and Sergeant Barnes dropped in. He showed up once more under that pretense before dropping it. A long stretch of days and weeks, then. A blunder of them. In memory, time collapses. Time-that-was and time-that-will-be become simply *then*. Months are a single hour, years a single long day.

B.H. had started off as a good man at heart, I think, once upon a time. Believed in his job, in what he was doing, in himself. But he was like others who deal poorly when things don't go as they think things should. When that happened, he felt his world unraveling, loose ends flying every which way. That grinds on year after year, you see the worst of people day by day, you change. And you could see that in his eyes, sense it coming off his skin like the alcohol haze from drinkers. It made you sad for the loss of the man he had been.

And when finally you come face to face with it, it can make you the kind of scared that never goes away.

I didn't give much thought to B.H.'s telling me Dan

might be in the area, but a week shy of our conversation about him, there Dan was, on his butt in the hallway leaned up against the wall with his legs straight out, when I got home one morning from work. Hair clipped close to the skull now, modest beard showing tufts of gray.

"How was Mobile?"

"Hot. Sloppy wet."

"And New Orleans?"

"The same. You been checking up on me?"

"What do you want, Dan?"

Susie cracked the door of her apartment to peer out, nodded when she saw me, and shut it.

"Just to say hi, for now. See how you are."

"Tired is how I am. And pissed. So get the fuck away from me."

He returned a couple of times in future weeks, once waiting at that same hallway spot when I got home from work, later outside the restaurant itself, both times making what might be construed as overtures, or just as easily as threats. Then he was gone. No big surprise, right? That's what he did. Came and went. Never knew what he had in mind.

Weeks later, I told B.H. about the visits. We were in the kitchen fixing dinner, me chopping and tearing and sorting for salad, him cooking creole food he'd learned from the woman who raised him after his mother died, a stew you'd swear would glow from inner heat if the lights went off.

"He didn't come back after that."

Without looking up he said, "You didn't tell me."

"Sorry. I should have."

"It's okay, I knew." Using a towel as holder, he set the pot on the cooling rack. "He won't be back."

"Caught—or just gone again?"

"Gone. You mind dishing up the rice?" He poured wine for us both. "He hurt people, Sarah, killed one we know of. Things like that, they can come back on you, from a direction you don't expect."

That's when I understood. I knew what had happened to Dan. Knew that for months B.H. had kept me close thinking Dan might at some point make contact. So many things started falling into place. That first visit, what had gone down with Susie and Bud next door. Bruises and abrasions on B.H.'s hands. His constant talk about pieces of dirt, human waste, and people going out the way they lived. Sergeant Barnes's request for a change in partners. B.H.'s friend on the force, Pryor Mills, and all those stories.

And I recognized my own willful ignorance. With alarms screaming and don't-do-it angels dancing on my shoulder, knowing what he was becoming, knowing what he was, I'd plunged ahead, stayed with the man, married him, pretended.

Looked away for so long.

Leave a violent man, you do it fast and hard, and you put as much distance between the two of you as quick as you can. B.H. knew nothing of my military background. And until the day I left, regardless the provocation, I'd never once became physical. The look of surprise on his face when I did, my own astonishment at what I was doing—both were like stones taking form in the air above us moments before crashing to earth.

I was in the bathroom getting ready for bed, eight or so in the morning, when he got home. He stood in the doorway watching, then stepped up behind me and put his hands around my neck. Gently at first, so it's possible that he meant it playfully, or thought he did. But every instinct within me, everything I felt in that moment, clicked on the latter. I had the hairbrush in my hand. I spun around and drove the handle into his throat.

Put your opponent down. If he can't breathe, he can't fight.

Then, just to be sure, no planning to any of this, only instinct and the rush of all I'd overlooked now spilling from me, I bent over him, seized his head in both hands, and slammed it into the floor.

I put my jeans, sweatshirt and shoes back on, shoved a few things in my handbag, and was gone.

4.

It rained five days.

Not that it mattered much. Plague and influenza and jungle rot had all come for a visit and refused to leave. Calling this simply *a cold* would be far short of the mark and for all I knew might exact, in retaliation, still more suffering. My breathing sounded like a very old, very leaky accordion. I was leaking, myself—everywhere. Or dripping. I smelled bad. Awful things were living in my mouth. My eyes refused to focus. Heart and head pounded. I was barely aware where I was.

Rain slamming at the window and taking away the rest of the world was a good audio-visual for how I felt.

The third day, I hauled myself to the kitchenette, a voyage of a hundred miles or so, to brew and drink a cup of bouillon, which I threw up before I got back to bed. Back to couch, rather, on which I'd ensconced myself with blankets, towels, tissues, paper towels, ice packs, various kitchen pots and pans as receptacles. The next time I got up, I fell twice on my way to the bathroom.

Breathing, balance, bowel movements—we take so much for granted.

People came and went around me. Some leaned over me to stare, others were just voices and never took shape. There was an ostrich once. Kids putting on some kind of play that involved lederhosen and cowboy boots. Under the sound of the rain, I kept hearing music I could never quite make out.

On the sixth day, the sun rose and so did I. Steam from the wet ground outside, stench and stagger from me. But I made it to the shower without major incident, and from there to the diner at the corner, shakily, for scrambled eggs.

Coming in, I'd noticed a woman sitting at one of the booths with a laptop. Familiar somehow. I took a seat at one end of the counter, as far from fortunate healthy folk as I could get, and, waiting for food, turned for a second look. I took in the way she held herself, the high cheekbones, hollow cheeks and black, shiny hair, how the musculature on her left arm was less defined than the right. After a moment, her head came up and her eyes met mine.

"Marta?"

She had the same problem I'd had: Who *is* this? Then—I could see—she got it. "Jesus, you look like hell."

"Pretty much where I've been the past five days. *You* look great." Nice skirt, classic blouse, both a good fit. And while I couldn't see them, heels must be under there. Hair cut short but not too short. Definitely not a QuikCuts special.

I told her about the plague.

She nodded. "Anything you walk away from, right?"

"We walked away from a few."

"Join me?"

"No fear of the plague?"

"We've been through worse."

Back in country, Marta and I'd gone through driver training together. Not that we were close, but the two of us were noticeably *there*, paying attention, while others, from their apparent indifference, might well have been hibernating. She'd broken that arm falling off the garage roof as a child. Four surgeries and a shitload of physical therapy later, it was almost as good as the other.

Talk of the good old days (which weren't) ran out quickly. We really hadn't spent loads of time together back then, or had that much in common, and over there, either nothing happened for days on end or all at once everything did. Not a lot left to say about that. And she wasn't any more inclined than I was to revisit it.

When she asked what I'd been up to since, I didn't know how to answer. I started with a story about coming home, a relationship or two, cooking, moving around, and went on from there, making up details as I went along.

And her? Looked as though she'd done well for herself, I said.

"It took some time. I was a mess. Lost every job I had, picked the worst men I could find—or who could find me. That whole first year I was drinking hard. Wake up mornings with no memory of what happened the night before, what day it might be, where I was. Then I came up with this . . . I don't know . . . this trick. Every time I felt like doing something stupid, I'd go back and remember what I'd seen there, bring up the memory of some horrible event or another, focus on the faces of those who never came back, or came back in pieces. Always made me feel bad about that, like I was using them, but it worked. I got myself straightened out, worked till I had enough money to go back to school full-time."

And now?

"I'm a paralegal. With a firm that mainly represents civil rights violations and discrimination suits. Funny how things change. I grow up in this strict, religious family, generations of board-certified conservatives, male-female and racial roles clearly defined, and here I am working day after day with the ACLU, unions, the Southern Poverty Law Center. Daddy's little girl's—grown up all right, but look what else happened."

By then I'd finished my eggs and three cups of hot tea and it felt as though everything was going to stay down. But if *I* stayed down any longer, it was going to turn out different. What little energy I'd had available was tapped out. They'd be forced to come in and scoop me out of the booth, throw me over one shoulder in a fireman's carry.

I remember looking down at my hand on the table, seeing it as though it were someone else's, as though at any moment it might startle and flee, scurrying across the table.

Marta and I made the usual sounds about seeing one another again, but they rattled with emptiness. Three days later I was in a geriatric Dodge Dart, the cheapest car I could find, and it rattled too, moving westward.

5.

Crows, it turns out, are very interested in death. Drop a crumpled sheet of black paper or plastic on the ground and they'll assemble, keeping it in view, sometimes for hours, before approaching. Come among them holding one of their own dead and they'll avoid you, scold, dive bomb. They'll remember your face. In the presence of a dead crow, gathered in groups as they are, they seem to be mourning. Scientists believe they're studying death, what it is and how it happens—that they are learning to understand it.

And so we go on.

And I come up somewhere in the middle of the country, somewhere toward the middle of my life, lying beside a man named Yves who's composing, with a single sharp breath between each, epitaphs that might grace our tombstones.

Gotcha!

The Worrying's Over.

That's all? That's it?

Sarah's Gone Missing.

Yes, all cheerful we are, as sunlight steams in at the open window following an earlier downpour and wind fingers the curtains.

Then he tells me about the crows.

Yves could easily have won contests for Gentlest Man Alive and Most Likely to Succeed. But his tongue was every bit as keen as his demeanor was sweet, his nature was that of a sprinter. By the time we met, he'd started four companies and got them going strong only to walk away. His interest flagged the moment a thing got built.

Each morning those slow, timeless days I'd watch him go to the window and stand, as though he were sniffing at the air, sifting through silent messages for intimations of what the day might bring.

He'd laugh at my description of the morning ritual, of course.

And laugh he does, turning back from the window, looking first at me, then with mock surprise at the erection due south.

Oh dear. Look what's happened.

The yard (I see now, as he steps out of the window frame) taken over by butterflies.

Those became—with no planning whatsoever, as so

often happens in life—the years of higher education. I was working as baker for a faux boulangerie near the college. Wasn't ever much of a baker, really, but I could fake it, same way the boulangerie did. Baby baguettes, popovers, croissants, cream horns, tarts. In by 4 A.M. to prep, through for the day by ten. Seeing students with their book bags, laptops and comfortable shoes, I got the notion to go back to school, and to maybe stay this time. I'd tried it a couple of times before and it never took.

Most of the students were half my age, the instructors not much closer. Everyone called me Miss Pullman. An advisor suggested that I start out slow, taking classes of particular interest to me, so I did. Like English 250: Life Themes, readings from world literature on a webwork of the great questions—death, individualism and community, the nature of reality—bolstered with compositions from twenty-year-olds about their own fascinating lives. Or American History: Unfolding the Narrative, which might well have been titled Remedial Thinking. Everything we are taught is false, the instructor told us the first day. Quoting Arthur Rimbaud, I'd later learn.

Don't expect miracles here, I certainly didn't. Lives rarely go into the oven as goo and come out beautifully golden. So, no boom or big bang, no moment when the frame freezes on a closeup, eyes clear and bright as the sound track throbs with meaning. Rather, a seepage. Slow waters coming in under the door, misplacing old toys and rugs and favorite shoes.

Can we choose who we are?

Can we choose what we believe?

Are those two questions blood kin?

To what extent are beliefs determined by choice, to what extent by the circumstances of our birth and, by extension, what we're exposed to?

And that's just—that was for me—the beginning.

Dr. Balducci taught by quotation and discussion. He'd start with something like what Rimbaud said, dangle it out across the room for discussion, eventually come back to the quotation's source and what it meant in that particular time, that particular life. Always the particular, he said, always. Abstractions will hold a pillow over your face till you die. There is no theory of everything. There is no theory of anything.

My favorite quote, the one I come back to most often? *Ask who benefits, and from whom.* Lenin. Try reading the latest statement from your politician, millionaire TV evangelist or corporate CEO through *that*.

A third-generation Italian-American, Dr. Balducci carried his pedigree with him. Still got shivers when he heard accordions, he said, still had family sitting on stoops and playing dominoes on sidewalk card tables back in Brooklyn, though "I do seem to have misconstrued the whole wise guy thing, going for my PhD." When he found out what I did, he told us about his grandparents' bakery, family-owned to this day, and the following week brought in Italian cookies for the class. He confessed that he'd been trying for most of his adult life to get through Dante's *Divine Comedy* in Italian. Kept giving it a go, he said, kept getting bogged down. The copy he brought in bristled with Post-its, each inscribed with the date he'd fetched up there in the dark woods with Dante, *Nel mezzo del cammin di nostra vita.*

Second year at the college, History of the Novel, I'm reading *Frankenstein*, finding out it's not at all the book I thought it was.

"Cursed and forever alone," Yves says, "its soul in torment, the monster tears apart its birthplace and flees into the countryside, right?"

"More or less."

"But that's not the end, that's never the end."

"No."

"Every novel, every poem, is the same single story, one we go on telling over and over again. How we try to become truly human, and never succeed."

Cheerful we were not, that night.

Often when things happen you realize you've felt them coming for a long time.

I was just getting home from class when Adrian, Yves's

partner in the new alternate-energy business, called. His secretary had walked into Yves's office and found him sitting erect and smiling before his desk computer, methodically erasing company files.

At the hospital I learned that by law I couldn't be given information on his condition and in fact, unmarried, had no standing at all. Yves, they told me, was under observation. They'd alert me if and when I might be admitted to see him.

That happened four hours and pocket change later, in a creepy, bare room on the eleventh floor. You buzzed to be let into that wing. The entrance doors were at the end of a long day room, and when the buzzer sounded, all heads turned from the TV to look. Most turned back. Some followed as you walked with the nurse who'd come to the door to meet you.

Yves sat, eyes dull, in a plastic chair whose color put me in mind of spoiled eggplant. He said something with muted gutturals, tried again and got out, "Stupid, huh?"

"On a scale of all else that happened around the world and in Washington today, barely a one."

"So hard to make an impression these days." He pointed to a window opening onto the nurses' station. Posters with inspirational sayings hung beside it, edges curling. "They're watching, to be sure you don't slip me drugs. Or worse. And by the way, you have two heads."

"In which case it sounds like you've had drugs enough."

"Could be. I feel unbelievably calm, and at the same time that I'm about to leap from my skin." He was silent a moment. "Interesting."

If he wanted to talk about it, he would. I knew that. So we sat quietly, which minutes later brought a face to the window. I nodded and smiled. He shot her the finger.

"They think they have all the answers."

"And you?"

"Not a single lonely pitiable one."

We went on sitting quietly until the nurse who owned the face at the window came in to tell me it was time to go. I asked her about visiting hours. Told Yves I'd see him after work tomorrow and said, "We'll get through this."

He laughed.

In memory that laughter resounds through the blur of following weeks, home from work, stop off at the hospital, make classes, shove in a wee wedge of sleep, circle back to the hospital, study there or at home, try for another wedge, go in, prep and bake, repeat. By the time Yves came home, just over seven weeks, there was little laughter left.

I'd leave for work or school with no idea what the day might bring. Serial phone calls for no reason. A ravaged house, as though large animals had been at play, upon return. A great abiding blankness.

For all of one week he rarely got out of bed. Another he spent watching a channel showing only vintage sitcoms, Danny Thomas, Dick Van Dyke, Joey Bishop, *I Dream of*

Jeannie, *Hazel*, and eating nothing but bread toasted with Velveeta.

In early April, seven weeks in, the therapist he was seeing (or mostly missing, since Yves canceled half the appointments) recommended that he return to the hospital for evaluation. They used that word a lot. Evaluation.

"Not to worry," Yves said, "back in a jiff. A quick tune-up. Tighten bolts, check belts, blow out the carburetor—start 'im up!" The old Yves peeking out for a moment from deep inside.

Ensuing months brought two further hospital tune-ups, new psych and behavioral therapists, and a barrage of drugs, though I was never sure how many of these he really took. Early on, I was peripherally involved in therapy. One session, the dead-serious therapist and dead-stubborn Yves sat staring at each other the whole hour. With another, a handsome possibly transgender woman, he wouldn't stop talking. Then there was the time he became a movie critic, responding to each question or comment with talk of plot dynamics and structure, the word *storyboard* surfacing frequently.

I'd felt the confusion and pain of others many times in my life, but had never been part of an anguish so absolute that it bleached all color from the world. Making the least decision had become insurmountable. The scales on which choices are made were out of commission. Everything was paper wrapping that came undone when you touched it.

One day in November Yves had been sitting staring out the window, me beside him reading for class. He turned to me and after a moment said, "The truth is up there, everything we need to know, written on the wall. I can read it, I just can't ever remember what it says once I look away."

Then he asked me about the book I was reading.

Not long after, I come home from work, the door's unlocked, the house is crazy neat. Cushions pushed into place on the divan, chairs at the kitchen table squared away, windows above the sink wiped clean. It's been one of those days my sponge won't bubble right, the gluten doesn't develop as I knead, dough takes twice as long to rise, and if I'm not at wit's end, that's the next stop on the train.

The day before, as everyone filed out of class, Dr. Balducci had asked that I stay behind. Your work is excellent, Ms. Pullman, no problem there. He slipped his book bag over one shoulder. John Updike called it signaling through the glass, he said. You stand up here looking out on all the faces, and sometimes you know, you sense, that something's wrong. You run the catalog in your mind: That this is none of your business. A breach of privacy even to bring it up. No relevance to the course or why we're here.

But I suspect, he said, that if I'm picking up on this, others are too. Perhaps you'd want to be aware of that.

Dr. Balducci lifted a hand, knocked with one knuckle at the invisible wall.

Yves was in the bedroom, pill bottles and bourbon on the

table alongside. He hadn't thrown up yet but did just as I came in. What came out was nasty, full of plastic, and bits of pill, and stink. I turned him on his side, checked and found a thready pulse, called emergency services. Once they'd come and loaded him aboard, I packed my single suitcase and drove to the train station. I called the hospital from there, but they wouldn't tell me anything. In the background I could hear phones ringing, alarms, anonymous voices.

Years earlier now. Nothing but police shows on TV, it seems, Latin America the hot spot for politics. I couldn't have quoted Rimbaud or Lenin if you held me down with a broken bottle of mescal to my throat. I was baking pies and cakes at a mom-and-pop, meat-and-potatoes café, I'd gained twenty-six unwelcome pounds, I had as best friend the owners's gay son who'd gone off to the state college and come home with a marble bag full of grand ideas he was ever so eager to share.

When we can no longer distinguish corporate power from government power, he'd say, we're on our way to fascism. It's never a slide, always a creep. Add god power and media power to the mix, and there you are. Here we are. Fascism, but with control in the hands of big business rather than government.

Mussolini said that, he'd say, more or less.

And that was the beginning, I guess, of this store of quotes and misquotes I've lugged around like a cotton picker's sack the rest of my life. Wallace Stevens wrote that whereas an idea is one thing, words can always be found to replace it.

A quote, for instance.

All the TV cops had sad lives. Deep scars. Wounds. Dark suggestions lurked just offstage; flashbacks happened in soft focus or black and white, often the same one, or variations, again and again; confessions stumbled from mouths in the last five minutes. These scars and wounds were supposed to explain the cops' lives, account for everything they did, every single action, every single inaction. Why they drank their morning coffee out of a child's chipped bowl, went silent when someone used the word *periwinkle*, never carried money, had six pair of the same shirt and pants.

My own personal cop failed the TV test miserably.

Sullen, uncommunicative?

The man talked all the time, in full sentences, and they made perfect sense.

War-torn? Wounded?

Disgustingly happy. Solid, secure, *there*.

Alcoholic?

A middling addiction to coffee.

And driven? Well, okay, that part's true.

We met when he stopped me for a bad tail light. Not broken, he said, more like stuttering? The restaurant had over-catered a school reunion the day before and I was on the way to donate leftovers to a retirement home, had boxes of wee sandwiches, small but proud cakes and half-cups of potato salad stacked on the back seat. When he handed me the warning ticket and started away, I figured, Hey, there's enough to go around, and called after him. Asked if the guys at the station would like some food.

He opened one of the boxes I gave him.

What, no doughnuts?

I looked at his name tag then.

"*Random*? You've got to be kidding."

"My mother was a great believer in chance—and not much else."

Four days later he called, starting off by apologizing for using his position to intrude on my privacy, and hoped that I might agree to meet him for coffee, a drink, or dinner.

Why not all the above? I said.

That first play date lasted three hours, our second most of a weekend he had off. Within the month we were living together, first at his ground-floor apartment that felt like a neatly-kept bureau drawer, then at a larger one that came empty on the second floor of his complex. Decidedly on our way up, Random said, who can dispute it?

So there we were, me going in on the cusp, not quite late night, not quite early morning, doing my baked goods before the kitchen got busy and occasionally staying over to run the grill (keep my chops up) when Karl was a no-show, Random working some nights, some swing shifts or doubles, both of us sleeping when we could grab a few hours. Standing joke was: We pass one another in the hall long enough to wave. The two of us really should get together some time.

We live in snow globes, don't we? Pick them up, shake them, years swirl about us and settle. Scouted out by an upscale restaurant, no idea how this happened, I jumped track from coconut cream pies to patés and unpronounce-ables. Discovered the wondrous autonomy of online study and, for all my distrust of what everyone called *being con-nected*, got my degree. Took up mountain biking and left those twenty-six pounds behind on the trails. Cherished Random, though not at all, I insisted, randomly.

Then the night I lay watching car lights glint off leaves wet from earlier rain and the phone rang. Before, I'd come suddenly awake from dreams inhabited by brightly lit cor-ridors, empty apartments and shadowy interrogators and, unable to get back to sleep, turned on the radio that I kept set for just such sleepless nights to a local station featuring old-time radio dramas. Something about political intrigues and doomed love in ancient Rome, but I didn't hear much of it.

On what he called in as a routine traffic stop, Ran had been shot. The stolen car was left there at the scene; they never identified the shooter. Ran died before I got to the hospital.

6.

Here's where the story begins, I guess. After Yves. Long after Ran. However hard you stare at maps and plan, you rarely get where you think you're going. But sometimes stray pieces of your life come together, the way military service, that college degree I'd earned for no particular reason, and exposure to police work from living with Ran got strung together the day I walked through double doors on Hob Street and applied for work as a cop.

It was the first time I'd talked to anyone about the desert and how I got there, the skinny kid with the RPG and Oscar, and I still don't know why I did. But my mouth had developed a life of its own, and Cal Phillips, himself a veteran of (his words) one of those wars no one talks about anymore, listened. Said he knew I had the job half an hour before I did.

I'm not about to claim there wasn't down time. No right angles in nature, few straight lines in life. I didn't walk out of the hospital and halfway across the continent into Cal's office. Lot of rough roads and mornings on the way. But I'm not going to fill in the blanks here, or try to pretend everything connects. It doesn't.

By then I was living in Farr, the kind of place that has period gingerbread houses shouldered up against modern cookie-cutters, where hardware stores and gas-and-live-bait shops cling to town's edge, where you hear the whisper of old-country vowels in local speech. Legend had it that there'd once been twin towns but Nearr had up and moved away. The night before I went to see Cal, I lay in bed with the radio turned low thinking about Yves's anguish, Ran telling me his mother believed in chance and not much else, Daddy saying we're from good hillbilly stock, we don't call police, we take care of things ourselves. I was seriously low on money and sorely in no mood to cook.

Once I'd run on and on and finally down, Cal said, "I've got a list of questions here. Supposed to ask you why you want this job. What are your best qualities. Where do you see yourself being in ten years. Screw all that. You want some coffee? Let me tell you about our town."

When we were done, he pointed one impossibly long ebony finger to a poster on the wall behind me. It showed a pile of rags and stray belongings—could there be a person under there?—in an alleyway. "I do have one question," he said. "What do you think about that?"

IN THE TIME YOU'VE BEEN DISCUSSING
THE LATEST CELEBRITY'S TUMMY TUCK
44 VETERANS HAVE COMMITTED SUICIDE

I turned back to him. I was empty, and just shook my head. He told me I had the job.

The house sat back off the street, plain white and unadorned, from simpler times when, mistakenly or not, we understood the American dream to be collaborative rather than competitive. Remains of a brick barbeque pit clung to the side yard along with a picnic table that looked as though the legs on one side had been gnawed at by an industrious beaver. Clap the salad bowl down at the high end and catch it at the low as it slid. A well-used Dodge in the driveway put me in mind of a dog whose master wouldn't take it for the walk it badly needed.

For days a neighbor had witnessed no activity, no coming or going, no sequence of lights, drapes or blinds, decidedly uncommon as Mr. Patch had always been regular as clockwork. When she went over to check on him (which is what neighbors do, right?) the mailbox was full, a FedEx package wedged between screen and front door. No answer when she rang the bell.

Nor was there any response when I rang, knocked, and called out, "Sheriff's Office." I tried the door. Locked, but the frame was old wood that gave when pushed against hard. The lock tore through. From deeper within came music, lightly festive, almost bubbly, strings and a horn or two.

I went toward the music, through the front room, down a hall hung with blue-green seascapes and sepia photos of people in clothing and hair styles from the forties, to the bathroom.

What struck me upon entry was the stillness, the repose. The peacefulness of it all. Clawfoot tub full to within inches of the top, water long gone cold, radio on a shelf to the side by neatly stacked towels and washcloths. The open Pabst Blue Ribbon beer on the shelf had not been drunk from. The tub's ancient enamel was chipped away on the rim, paint of much the same color peeling from the wall behind. Mr. Patch leaning back as though he'd only fallen asleep there.

Something about the wash of light from the window above and to the left of the tub, the spill of shadow, stirred memories of . . . what? Took me a moment to pull it up: *Intro to Art History*, elements of classical painting. Mannerist structure, the distribution of light and shadow across the canvas, hand pointing up to the heavens, hand pointing down to earth—that sort of thing. How the central figure (as Dr. Warren in baggy khakis and bright Hawaiian shirt explained) becomes at once individual man and manifestation of some larger meaning.

Not that I could find some larger meaning here, or any meaning at all.

Certain images from our life stay with us, the lopsided crane we built from an erector set when we were ten, the dried husk of a pet chameleon, scenes from *Rashomon* or *Attack of the Fifty-Foot Woman*, and we don't know why. Do these, like dreams, derive from random firings of synapses? Or is there something about them freighted with meaning—veiled messages from universes within ourselves?

Often at night, after this, I'd put on baroque music. Horns and strings, Telemann maybe, or Steinmetz. Didn't matter. It's the pulse I was looking for, the way the music's so alive, so continuous.

That first sight of the room remains with me today, indelible. I imagine Mr. Patch preparing his bath, choosing his music, opening the beer. Then leaning back and, in absolute repose, in absolute peace, dying. As though the world in that moment, for that moment, held its breath.

Very few lives end in such grace.

Nine months in the saddle, almost ten, when I caught the call, by which time I'd been through my fair share of bar fights, domestic disturbances, runaway kids—the standard small-town B-list. Plus a handful of assaults, a shotgun suicide, a fatal hunting accident. But this was one that stayed with me.

When I began asking about, nobody knew much of Mr. Patch's life. He'd shown up maybe thirty years ago, paid cash for the home he died in. Kept to himself, no sign of family or friends, near as anyone could recall. One name did come up: Riley or Raleigh Robinson, living as a squatter in the ruins of an old mansion in what was once rich farmland between Farr and Johnstown. With help from an ageless attendant at the filling station where I stopped for a coke so cold there was ice in its throat, and from a kid I came across walking abandoned railroad tracks, I found my way.

In its glory days the place could have put up three families and they'd have no need to mingle. Now walls, floors and doorframes skewed off at cockeyed angles every which way and the skirt of the wraparound porch sagged around the home's ankles, dragging ground. The first couple times I went out there, stood on the porch and knocked, nothing came of it, though I could hear movement inside. No way one could walk those wood floors silently. Shift weight and parts of the house shift with you. Third time, the door opened. I could smell frying meat inside. Not very good meat.

His skin was mottled, patches of it black, others milk-chocolate, the palms of his hands pink-white and deeply creased. Both hands shook.

"You just don't give up, do you, Miss?"

"Not much anymore, no sir, I don't."

"Whatever you're looking for ain't here."

"It's about Willis Patch."

"He ain't here either."

"I came to tell you he died."

No pause. "The hell you did." Nothing showed on his face or in his eyes. "Ain't nobody drives all the way out here, on what precious little's left of them damn roads, without she wants something. And she sure don't do that three times. But you might as well come on inside."

Motioning me to a saddlebroke couch of a shade of green not seen in nature, he went out to shut off the stove then sank into a chair so low that his knees stuck up level with his head. I told him who I was, about the call and my breaking into Mr. Patch's home. When I was done we sat there, spine and joints of the house creaking around us.

"Peaceful, you say." He shifted in the chair. One front leg of it was an inch shorter than the others. "That's good. Man survives almost ninety years, he's deserving of some peace."

"He didn't look to be close to that old."

"Willis was from hardy stock, tough people made tougher by the lives they lived."

"What can you tell me about him?"

"This in regard to tidying up your paperwork?"

"No sir." I tried to explain how Mr. Patch's death had made me feel. Sad. Calm. How little I understood of other lives. My sense of loss. I didn't do a very good job with my explanation. I haven't done much better since. Words just won't hold it all. But whatever I said, it prompted Raleigh or Riley (he'd said his name, I still couldn't be sure) to go on.

"Willis, he was a private man. Figured his business was his, just like others' business should stay theirs. Guess that don't matter so much now."

Willis Patch's father, he told me, hailed from St. Louis. He'd been a doctor there, Niggertown they called it back then, and did his best to take care of all he could. Went from house to house when need be, ran a clinic out of one-half of the family's living room. People used to say Dr. Patch had delivered half Niggertown's babies, then delivered *their* babies. There was talk of the riots, too—people remembered—with over a hundred injured put up in the basement at Holy Methodist, and Dr. Patch the only doctor to see after them.

Man died, maybe eighty years old, still going about his business. Dropped dead in the street late one night on his way to the colored hospital they had by then. And that's when they found out he hadn't been a doctor at all. Never had a license, never had one blessed day of schooling. Wife said he told her when he was just coming up he looked around and saw how bad the community needed doctors, so he decided right then and there to make one of himself. From books, he said. Read everything in the library, everything he could find, till he was half blind. Learned everything he knew from reading those books.

Which must have been in his blood, cause Willis was the same way. Whatever you brought up, whatever you asked about, Willis knew of it, or if he didn't he soon would.

By his mid-twenties he was living in D.C. When he found out in Virginia you didn't have to go to law school to be admitted to the bar, he talked a local lawyer into letting him read law with him for a year, that's what they call it, reading law. Studied his black ass off, he used to say, then took the big test.

He lawyered a long time, out of an office above a general store first, then out of one tucked away at the back of a beauty shop in another town a little closer, he said, to civil-eye-zation. Helped out a lot of folks. You had to wonder like I did how he scratched out any living at all for himself.

Back then's when we met up. Some woman's purse got snatched out front of the Safeway. Me being black and easy to find, they came and got me. I was cooking at Sally Ray's Homestyle Café, sleeping in the storeroom. Still don't know how he did it, but Willis got me right up before a judge. Hour later, they turned me loose. Ever so often after that, Willis'd come find me to see how I was doing.

Me, I never had much of anything by way of ambition, always been good with who and where I was, but Willis, he might have had too much of it. Like he was carrying 'round this load—all this and that that needed doing, and him coming to see how little of it gets done. One night he stopped in at the tire store where I was working to say good-bye. He'd brought sodas and sandwich fixings. The sack had smears on the side where grease from the meats soaked through. We sat out back eating. Plenty of grease back there too. You think you've got hold of it, he said, car's running smooth, not much noise under the hood, lights are good out there ahead of you. But the damn thing keeps breaking down. A mile outside town, a hundred, don't matter, it just keeps breaking down.

Lot of water under the bridge after that, can't begin to tell you how surprised I was to run into old Willis again. Told him now I had me a house too, and when he saw it he said my house like to had more potential than any he'd ever seen.

Years dragged by, way they will. We'd meet up time to time. Never asked him why it was he came to living up here, same as he never asked me. But Willis'd say things, you know. Like how some people seem put together different. Him living the way he did, keeping to himself, that had to do with something inside him he'd come to know. Told me one night he set out to change things but instead, things had changed him. I figure something must of happened, something to do with the law, but Willis never spoke on it.

"I appreciate this, Mr. Robinson," I said, standing.

"Don't know what you looked to find here, young lady."

Nor did I. The shorter chair leg tapped at the floor as my host also stood.

Mr. Robinson's stories rode home with me in the car. I made it back for my shift, got home around midnight, then lay awake till dawn.

It turned into one of those nights when the temperature

dropped five or six degrees and refused to budge further, so humid that lights went blurry and sheets got soaked. After a while I pulled mine off and put on clean ones; within the hour the new ones were as soggy as the old. A storm brewed far off—rumbles of thunder, flares of lightning at the edge of my vision—but it never came closer.

7.

All stories are ghost stories, about things lost, people, memories, home, passion, youth, about things struggling to be seen, to be accepted, by the living.

One morning I woke staring at the faded bamboo shoots on the wallpaper, went out to the kitchen to look for coffee, and found that I was acting sheriff.

By this time I'd moved to a small house outside town. Like Mr. Robinson's it had potential. Three rooms the size of flatbed trailers, fixtures replaced so carelessly that insects came and went around them as they wished, yawning gaps between doors and frames, kitchen cabinets hung such that one walked softly nearby. I didn't own a TV or radio, stayed away from the Internet, hadn't seen a newspaper in years. Now and again I'd overhear people talking about current events—bad guys and good guys implicit in what they were saying—and wonder anew that people could live in such uncomplicated worlds.

The beeper went as I was dumping coffee into the French press. KC, who had recently graduated from the local high school where he was star football player and who should have been off shift, answered when I called in.

"Sarah? It's about Cal."

Which could mean many things, but my mind filled in the blank with the worst.

"Ceci couldn't get him on the phone last night. This morning she went over there."

His daughter, one of those women who looked like a teenager well into her thirties, which she was, worked three towns over at some charity for kids, trolling the well-to-do for contributions. *Well-to-do* being distinctly relative hereabouts.

"He's missing," KC said.

No way missing sounded good, but it was on the list below, say, getting shot dead during a routine traffic stop. "Out of here last night at six, six-thirty, Bruno says. Never showed at The Elite." Where he had dinner, the daily special, something like 300 days out of 365.

"I'll be right in."

Clad and shod in record time, I'd backed out of the drive before realizing I had failed to pick up my Glock and was wearing two different boots, so I left the motor running and went back. The phone was ringing as I relocked the door but I let it go. I carried a cell as backup but as often as not forgot to turn it on. That's what I claimed, anyway. So everybody used the landline.

The drive into town was quietly reassuring. Bobbie Ferguson, feet barely able to reach the pedals, waved from the vintage Schwinn that had belonged to her granddad. The ancient tree by the town square, given up for dead most every year before it pushed out delinquent sprigs of green, was filling with leaves. Farr had limped from rural to urban long after much of the rest of the country, carrying history on its back with its brick and clapboard homes, narrow streets and town square. Years before, the town hall had been taken over by a Lutheran church. The gazebo in the square housed generations of feral cats.

KC came out the back as I pulled into the parking lot. Opened the passenger door and got in.

"Judge Polick says consider yourself sworn in."

"I've already been sworn in."

"As acting sheriff."

"I've been on the job a year, KC."

"Don't matter." He pointed ahead. "Left at Cypress."

KC's directions took us north to an imposing home that, plantation-like, stood on a hill as though southwest winds might have carried spores from it to spawn the town.

"This is where Cal lived?"

"So I'm told," KC said.

Ceci had given him a key and, crossing a covered porch that must once have held older folk seated on swings and gliders swapping stories as they watched youngsters play, we entered. The porch floor's hardwood tongue and groove continued into the entryway.

"Ceci says turn left off the hall."

And so we did, into what had no doubt been a dining room. The rest of the house, we soon found, was closed off.

"You've never been here before?" KC asked.

I shook my head.

"Doesn't look much like anyone has," he said.

A narrow bed, impeccably made, stood against heavy oak sliding doors. The doors were latched, their recessed handles, presumably the hidden clockwork as well, heavy brass. By one casement window a formica-topped table held a vertical file with half a dozen slots, and a letter tray. Between tray and file, flanked by a coffee mug bearing pens, scissors and stapler, Cal's phone and beeper charger were aligned. Gauzy curtains at each tall window.

"Place looks like a board game," KC said.

He was right. Table and bed holding the room in place, loveseat and Morris chair at complementary angles near its center, shoes squarely beneath the chair. More at work here than simple orderliness: move a single piece, the whole tangible world could tilt off plumb.

KC went to look through the house while I poked around there in the cockpit. A radio on the end table by the Morris chair played a local oldies station when clicked on. The chair's cushion was lumpy and faded to purple from who knows what original color. The battered loafers under the chair had been recommissioned as house slippers, heels permanently mashed in.

I shuffled through the folders. Bills paid early in batches, regular deposits to a savings account. Polaroids and photos of Ceci as a child, at school age, as gowned college grad. Medical records for the VA, private physicians, lab work, pharmacies. Tax forms. Sixteen personal letters, none of them over two brief paragraphs. Birth certificate, marriage license, Social Security card, Living Will.

At one point KC came back to tell me there was a boxed set of *Story of Civilization* in there, eleven books. I was surprised he knew what they were. "And a whole set of Encyclopedia Brittanica, when's the last time you saw one of those?"

"He had a kid, remember?" I said. "That's what people did."

On the drive back to town, I got a full report of the house's contents. Long-outdated food on kitchen shelves, unplugged refrigerator, clothing still in bags from the dry-cleaner, Ceci's room just as it must have been when she lived there as a teen, one toilet out of three, in the utility room by the kitchen, that remained functional, nest of wasps inside a broken window.

"Man lived in that one room, didn't he? With a whole house right there."

"Looks like," I said.

"Why would he do that, Sarah?"

I shook my head. Why people do most things is a mystery. Trying to keep it simple, maybe. Keep it on the surface. What you see is what's there.

"Will he come back?"

"We don't know that he's gone."

We didn't know jack.

How was it that the Cal we spent our days with and the Cal who lived in that room were the same person? And where were both of them, besides missing? I'd spent time myself doing my best to stay close to the wall, avoid taking on weight. Slipping away, keeping on the move. Private lives, public lives. We all have them. The unexamined life may not be worth living, but the examined life, any examined life at all, is for damn sure going to surprise, confound and disturb you. Still, here I am, writing this all down, just as I did in the spiral-bound notebook when I was seven.

"Where are you?" Brag asked. Brag from Bragley, the man himself attenuated like his nickname, barely five foot, but at ease with himself in a way few are. Brag was our go-to guy. Maintenance, vehicle upkeep, telephone answerer, supplies, dispatch, errands. Whatever was needed. Would have taken the computers apart and figured out how to fix them if we asked. None of us had any inkling back then that he'd wind up running the show.

We'd had rain most of the night. Steam rose from the

parking lot as the sun took hold. I held a cup of coffee I could remember neither pouring nor drinking, though it was near empty.

"Sorry," I told Brag. "Kind of on cruise control."

"Will Baumann called." Our mayor-slash-furniture tycoon, whose wife had died five years back in a traffic accident. Always felt myself going sly and slippery when around him, though I was never sure the apparent overtures were real. Maybe it was just that he wanted to stay in the game, sensed that flirting with me was safe. "Said come on down when you can and he'll buy you lunch. Wanting to pick your brain about Cal, you think?"

"Nothing much in there that's ripe."

"Unlike what's done spoiled in others?"

Classic Brag. The way he spoke matched his stature and nickname. He could sum up the Peloponnesian War in a sentence.

I'd gone back by myself to Cal's place one late afternoon days later and sat in the desk chair, trying to feel my way into his life, I guess. It was so quiet I could hear wasps at their work in the nest two rooms away. Sunlight pooled on the bed across the room and lapped onto the floor.

When quite young I was short and small for my age. Till I got my growth, got called Runt a lot, but Daddy never once used that nickname. Instead he built me a pair of wooden stilts so I could be, in my mind and in my secret life, taller.

Cal had done much the same for me.

Common wisdom says when you take on a job and don't know what you're doing, just keep your head down, keep plugging away, and you'll grow into it. Truth is, it's more like when you buy a dress a size too small thinking it'll push you to slough off a few pounds. Then the thing hangs in the closet for a couple of years before you toss it out or give it away. And that's what would have happened, in the job, in my life, if it hadn't been for Cal. I hadn't yet grown into job *or* life, but I didn't worry too much anymore about wearing them out in public.

I finished what was left in the coffee pot, did some paperwork, and met Will for lunch at the Gray Goose. No one remembered where the diner's name came from; I'd asked. Some did remember its serial pasts as a bar, Mexican cafe, polling place, and thrift store.

Will stood as I came to the booth, then dropped smoothly back in place as I took my seat. Most of his day consisted of sitting at a desk, getting up, retaking the desk. He had it down cold.

And he wanted an update, of course, on Cal.

I told him what we knew: abandoned house, one-size-fits-all room, toilets gone south, desk sorted, no sign of disturbance—quite the contrary, in fact. Everything at parade rest. I even told him about the wasps.

He looked disappointed. Had that down cold too.

"No cryptic message scrawled in blood on the desk," I said. "Sorry."

Our food came. Will's salad was the size of an African termite nest, healthful mound of chopped lettuce, carrots, cucumber and tomato undone by the ham, cheese, hard-boiled egg and globs of bottled dressing dumped on top.

"Square one, then." He added salt from the shaker, just to be sure.

"Come right down to it, we're still looking for square one. Maybe we saw it scooting around the corner—"

"So we have to rethink this."

A phrase, not an idea. Where Will lived, thoughts didn't lead to knowledge, they backstepped from what he believed he already knew.

He asked some more questions to which I had no answers and I got most of my tuna on toast down before Brag showed up to tell me I was needed in Boomtown.

Boomtown wasn't a town at all, but an accretion. A tide pool of sorts. Years ago migrants had moved into houses built for millworkers in the forties and long left unmanned. They'd shored these up with plywood and reclaimed lumber to make them liveable. Then one by one others joined them, some in trailers, some with hammer and nails, some with power tools, till we had a community of 200-plus perched there three miles outside town. It had become an active, stable community, rough and ragged yet well kept. But it was a community with none of the amenities of an actual town, without even a name. Garbage collection, access to water and electricity, maintaining streets, that sort of thing, residents worked out among themselves. With what they couldn't, even though the town had no obligation to do so, Farr helped out.

Davey, our newest add-on, had responded to a neighbor's phone call, then, given the situation, called in for me. What I found upon arrival was a tableau, three people standing in a kitchen posed as if for a movie still. By the stove and counter a fortyish man with tufts of hair like weeds in an empty lot held a skillet, a woman of similar age wearing denim overalls had a butcher knife in hand. Near the doorway a young woman (mid-length hair dyed black, straight skirt, print blouse) was backed against the wall.

"I asked them repeatedly to lower their . . . utensils," Davey said. "And to please stand down. They won't budge."

"Can someone tell me what this is all about?" I stepped closer to the woman. Her eyes never strayed from the man and his skillet. "Ma'am?"

Nothing.

"Is everyone okay?"

"Best answer the sheriff," Davey said.

At that, the woman looked my way. I kept watch on the man's feet in my peripheral vision as she thought about it, went back and forth, decided.

"Girl says she's his daughter."

"Okay, good. We're talking." I waited a couple of beats. "You live here in the house, ma'am?"

"Me and Karl."

"And you, miss, would you mind stepping outside with me?"

"Anything to get out of here."

I led her onto the porch, closing the door behind us. We moved a little farther along. Through a window I could see Davey talking to the couple inside. It wasn't much of a porch, just a floor and railing of rough planks tacked on, skeletal. A good crop of what looked like skunk cabbage showed through the floor's spacing.

"I'm Sarah."

"Toni. Thank you for rescuing me in there." She was looking around, house to house. "This is a strange place. Feels a lot like where I grew up, though."

"Not in these parts?"

"Up north, around Meyer."

Where, Cal once said in speaking of the state's diverse topography, the mountains first begin shrugging their shoulders.

Her eyes came to mine, moved away again. "I thought they were going to kill each other. We were standing there talking. She turned around and when she turned back she had that knife in her hand. He picked up the skillet. Started saying Ruth I'm sorry, over and over."

"For what? The skillet?"

"Or for me."

"Had you met the man before?"

"No, ma'am."

"But you say you're his daughter?"

She nodded.

"And that's why you came here today?"

"I'd talked myself out of it for a long time."

"What changed?"

Inside, Davey and the couple stood where they were before. Skillet and knife had been put aside.

"Never seem to know why I do things," Toni said, "even in the midst of doing them. Are other people like that?"

"Just about everybody I know."

"This time, this one time, I do know."

I waited.

"My mother told me about him eight years ago, when I was sixteen. She died last month. Ovarian cancer, back for the third time. I thought he might want to know."

"Then you aren't here—"

"There's nothing I want from him, no, ma'am."

"Did you tell them that?"

"They didn't give me a chance."

We went back in and, inasmuch as we could, squared things. The young woman, Toni, took off in her car, a mid-size blue Hyundai. I told Karl and Ruth that Davey or I'd be around the next day or two to check on them, be sure everything was okay. It was Davey who wound up going out there, only to find Toni back for a visit, the three of them sitting around in the kitchen drinking iced tea.

By the time I got to the office I realized I'd missed an

appointment to address graduating seniors at Burton High—Cal's standing gig, one he did every year—and called to reschedule. Principal Morley's assistant Miss Hester, not so much the heart of the school as the hard seed of it, grudgingly agreed to provide me a second chance. Her schedule was so full, you know. This was a terrible imposition on her time.

What was left unsaid, as ever, burning fiercely.

8.

That evening, light would not let go without a struggle. I'd personally given up on my day an hour before, checked out, picked up dinner at Cecil's on the way home. Now late sunlight clung to open spaces, walls and treetops, and stretched in a narrowing band along the horizon.

I was sitting out back with a mouthful of greens, trying not to think overmuch about dollops of bacon grease as seasoning or the mysterious bits of meat lodged within, when the phone rang. I'd remembered to turn the answering machine on, so it picked up. No message. The cell phone was in there too, probably turned off or uncharged.

I'd spent hours that afternoon, *spent* in the sense of exhausted or used up, in a meeting. Stu Coleman planned to purchase plots at town's edge for development and applied for rezoning and appropriate licensing; a meeting had been set up weeks earlier. I was stand-in, understudy, for Cal. And mostly I was recalling advice from him. When you don't know what's going on, stay quiet. When someone looks your way, be deep in thought.

I definitely didn't know what was going on, having heard about the meeting only the day before and the whole affair, from attending such meetings at all, right on up to zoning and talk of taxable revenue dollars, being as alien to me as frying up a mess of grasshoppers for dinner. But I did know that the property Stu Coleman had his eye on housed many of the town's poorest and that if they were vacated they'd have nowhere to go. Stu claimed that he'd build affordable housing for them elsewhere. Sure he would. Fortunately I wasn't alone in my misgivings. A solid row of disbelieving townspeople showed, eight of them. Following each statement from Stu, Mayor Baumann or council members, one of the contestors, starting far left and moving in orderly fashion along the row, would raise his or her hand to ask a question.

I'd gone inside to rinse the carry-out container when the phone rang again. This time, I beat the answering machine to it.

Brag.

"San Antonio mean anything to you?"

"Not that I recall. Why?"

"I'm in here fielding calls about Cal. So I pick up figuring this one's more of the same, and what I get is 'Sarah Pullman, please.'"

"Man or woman?"

"Man."

"Did he say anything else?"

"When might you be available. And no number or message, he'd call back . . ."

I waited.

"Felt wonky. Craziness, or like some weird code. I had the call back-routed to San Antonio."

"We can do that?"

"Phone company can, when you know the right person."

"Thanks, Brag."

"We're getting a shitload of calls about Cal. Anything particular you want us to say?"

"The usual. We're working on it."

"Are we?"

Doing what we can, I said. "Anything else?"

He let silence answer.

"Call me if."

"Got it."

Truth was, I didn't have a clue where to start, what to do. It felt as though a knot as hard and smooth as a bowling ball had been handed off to me and I had to sit there till I figured out how to untie it. I also wondered at something I had wondered at many times before: Did I bring bad fortune to people I was close to? Mother, Oscar, Yves, Random. The baby. Now Cal.

But to really think that, you had to have some kind of closed belief system, didn't you? Once when I was a kid, a visitor to the house who'd had a regular marathon of bad stuff come down on her said *Everything happens for a reason*, and before I even knew I was going to speak up, moments before Daddy sent me from the room, I told her that had to be the stupidest thing I'd ever heard, a pitiful attempt to make herself feel better.

Some things just happen.

Still, once you start poking at the past it gets hard to stop.

Next day, I left the office for what started as a routine ride about town (might as well check out that property Stu Coleman was after, while I was at it) and found myself an hour later on the old two-lane highway that once ran up to the capitol, nowadays crumbling, half sunk into the ground, and used only for access to the city dump. More to the point, it ran directly away from Farr, and I had no reason to be there, miles from town.

How many lives had I walked or driven away from by now?

I turned off onto State Road 61 and passed an abandoned farm with remnants of house and barn and a scatter of chickens who'd stayed on or been left behind.

I spent a lot of time among chickens back when we raised them. Everything that could be automatic, was—food and water dispensers, timers in the gas brooders, heat lamps—but the equipment continually needed upkeep, and six thousand chickens put out a lot of droppings. Three chicken houses, each of them 75 x 25 feet. That's many a pound and square yard of wood chips that need turning. And many a fifty-pound sack of food to be hauled in.

The chickens are where it came together for me. I don't know exactly when, but I was still small enough to climb through the hole in the Bishops' fence, so eight or nine maybe. I sat down to pee. A beetle about the size of a black bean was walking—I thought—at the seam of wall and floor. But as I watched I realized it wasn't walking along the wall, it was walking *into* the wall. It would hit, stand still a moment before backing away and turning in a circle, then walk into the wall again. The beetle did this over and over, never straying from a two-inch-square area. It had goals, a plan, it wouldn't give up.

Everybody believes we're different from the others, the dogs, cats, giraffes, insects. That these act only on instinct, guided by reaction to basic needs. The next day, out among the chickens again, I decided everybody was wrong. That beetle had consciousness. A sense of itself as an individual being. So did the chickens. They experience pain, fear, confusion. Sick or damaged, they struggle not to die, to go on. They plan. They try. They *hurt*. Ours would know three places in the world: where they were hatched, our houses, the slaughterhouse. Not much of a life. And in a child's all but wordless way, I began to wonder how different our own might be.

I'd been moving steadily away from Farr, thoughts

stacked in my head like layers of brittle shale, surprised anew at the number of abandoned farms and small homes. Sometimes it seems like everything is shutting down, the whole world going gray at the edges.

At the next crossroad, I turned and headed back.

9.

I spent the rest of the morning on the phone, calling every police and sheriff's department in this part of the state. We had a bulletin on Cal out to all agencies, and alerts to area newspapers and broadcasters, but I wanted to add a human voice to the mix. Even dialed the local FBI up at the capitol. Mostly those guys seem to be accountants and lawyers of one sort or another. The one I got was a clerk who would have made Russian bureaucracy circa 1900 proud. I'm pretty certain he was reading from a playbook. I'd ask a question or make a statement, there'd be a pause followed by a perfectly grammatical response that had maybe thirty percent relevance to what I'd said. I fought off the urge to see how far I could push it, thanked him, and hung up.

I was getting ready to grab a late lunch when Sammy Brocato called. Sammy owned and ran a warehouse, mostly supplying restaurants, and weekly inventory had come up short. No sign of a break in, but enough was missing that he had to suspect theft. A dozen cases of canned soups, another couple dozen of vegetables, corn beef hash and peaches. We're not talking bigtime felons here, Sammy said, but if stuff's walking out the back door with someone, especially if it's with any of my people, I need to know.

Unlike Cal's disappearance, this was something I could handle. Ask questions, leave space and silence and let it fill—almost always worked. Two hours and seven conversations later, it did. Sammy, who saw pretty much everything as commerce of one sort or another, carried around a powerful dislike of churches, said they lay claim to helping the people and the community while milking both. Sammy's wife used to go along with his thinking, but after their eldest child got killed in a traffic accident some months back, Eileen returned to the Methodist church she'd been brought up in. Everyone knew storms had set down between them; once I started asking questions, that came out.

By the time I got to her, Eileen admitted she'd given the food to a meals-for-homeless program at the church. Hadn't asked Sammy because she knew even if he didn't say no she'd never hear the end of it, so she'd spoken to the nightshift foreman, an old friend, and begged his help.

I left Sammy and Eileen to work it out on their own and settled down at Mindy's to eat. Wind was kicking up devils of dust and debris in the street outside. Predictably enough, when three strong gusts in a row hit, doors got rattled and alarms went off at Sheldon's Hardware. The store had been closed for close on to three months following Ed's diagnosis with cancer, leaving us all to wonder if it would reopen. Meanwhile the poor fit of doors and windows in the ancient building, one of the oldest on Farr's main street, guaranteed alarms with any high winds or storm. We were used to it, didn't think much about it, but I asked Mindy's kid to hold my food for me while I strolled down to be sure.

Late that afternoon, another Farr-sized crisis arrived with a call from the Mars Bar. We got there, Davey and me, to find two men, neither of whom we knew, standing among the UFOs, spacemen and monster figurines Burl had tucked away on shelves, beams and pretty much every available unused surface, swearing and giving forth declarations of what they were going to do to each other, an entire bar fight waged in the future tense, as though they'd caught strains of some futuristic affliction from the toys and models surrounding them.

We sent them on their way and went back to the office, Davey to log our visit and fill out the shift report, me to look again through my notes regarding Cal. No sudden revelations. No return on my investment of morning calls.

It was dark when I got home, clouds clinging to the rim of a bone white moon, a knock at the door.

This far out, there weren't many neighbors. Clara Holden was one of four, a woman who respected privacy as much as I did, and the first person I ever knew to make a living selling on the Internet. She had on what was for her business casual. Oversize jeans with legs rolled up, sneakers with no socks, sweatshirt.

"Sorry to bother you, Sarah. Any chance you're having work done on the house?"

I told her no, I was afraid it would look the same the next time she came over. Or worse.

"Which'll be like a year from now, yeah, I know. Not that—"

"I understand, Clara."

"Of course you do."

"Would you like to come in?"

"Need to get back. But." She gestured behind her, the way she'd come. "About two this afternoon I glanced up from doing dishes and saw a man walk out from behind your house. Not something I'd seen before, or would expect to."

"Could you see what was he doing?"

"Looking in windows, checking the house out. That's when I thought just maybe . . ."

I shook my head.

"No reason to be here, then."

"None."

"Right. So I grabbed my phone and got a picture."

Not all that much to see when she handed it to me. Male, six feet tall reckoning by scale comparison to the house, give or take an inch. Medium build. Brown slacks or what we used to call chinos, dark shirt, gray windbreaker, ball cap.

I handed the phone back. "No vehicle?"

"Not that I saw. Give me your email, I can send this to you."

"You'll have to send it to the office."

"Will do."

"Thanks, Clara."

"And I'll keep an eye open."

I grabbed a flashlight and went out to look around as she headed home. Wouldn't you know it, no rare cigarette ash, no size 14 narrow shoeprint with one-of-a-kind tread. I made my way through trees and brush to the old farm road. A vehicle with wide tires and a slight oil leak had been parked there recently, but that could be anything. Anyone.

The phone was ringing as I came back inside but stopped before I could get to it. I called the office to be sure it wasn't them, then got coffee started. I'd taken the first bite of an apple when the phone rang again, and when I set the apple down to answer, a roach poured over the lip of the sink to claim it. The roach was looking pretty happy (what a windfall!) by the time I said hello and Cal asked if I was all right.

For a moment I couldn't respond, so many questions cascaded in my mind. Are *you* all right? Where are you? Why?

"Okay, considering," was what I settled for.

"That's good. Figured you got railroaded into taking over."

"They didn't even ask."

"They usually don't." In the silence I could hear a low buzzing on the lines. "You'll do fine."

"That sounds . . ."

"Final? Not much is. Things get smaller in the rear view mirror but they don't go away."

"People do."

"Sarah . . ."

I waited.

"I did things, a long time ago—when I first got back. I was messed up. Really messed up. The Cal that's around now and the one around then, they just can't be in the same place at the same time, not any longer."

"I think I understand."

"People are going to wonder. There'll be stories, all kinds of stories—if there aren't already. Blanks don't sit well with us, we like to fill them in. Have to."

"Just tell me you're all right."

"Getting there, Sarah—isn't that what we're all trying for?"

"On our best days."

"Take care, my friend."

"Cal—"

But he was gone.

On our way back from Cal's place three days before, KC asked me a question I'd been carrying around ever since.

We'd come down the hill and turned toward the old highway, both of us quiet. As we swung around a bend, we slammed into ruts, sending dozens of blackbirds from trees to sky.

"Do you have friends, Sarah?" KC said.

Naturally, people had to wonder. Lived out where I did, kept to myself, never talked about my past. Right there in front of them, and at the same time not quite.

"Mostly from years ago," I said.

Silence stood on tiptoe, two beats, before it came down.

"Back in the day, right," KC said. "I had all kinds. The other jocks, cool girls. Hell, even a nerd or two. But senior year something changed. Same people, same hanging out but . . ."

KC sat looking out the window on his side. Birds had settled back into trees. "We have to keep moving, don't we? That's the secret."

KC was the last person I'd have figured for a philosophical bent, but people are rarely what we think they are. Dr. Balducci: *Always the particular. Abstractions will hold a pillow over your face till you die. There is no theory of everything. There is no theory of anything.* And yet we seem hardwired to reach for those abstractions.

"Sorry, Sarah. That got to me, back there."

"The loneliness of it?"

"More how orderly it was, when I think about it. Everything in its place. The lack of clutter. All the lives I know are messy."

10.

Back my sixth day as a cop in Farr, a Lincoln Town Car came down Walnut Street at what was later determined by Highway Patrol investigators to be just over 65 mph and crashed into Sutton Drugs. Like everyone else downtown, we heard it. Cal and I were in the office going over procedures and paperwork. By the time we got outside, most of the rest of the town were already out there looking to see what had happened.

Half the storefront was gone. The Lincoln's trunk and tail stuck out. Pieces of the store's plate glass window lay everywhere, painted-on letters showing on some, an S, a DR. The ceiling and roof directly above sagged onto the car.

"That way," someone said without Cal asking—the mayor, I'd later learn. He pointed around the side of the building. An improvised alleyway back there where businesses put out garbage bins for pickup, then twenty yards or so to the treeline.

We found him barely into the trees, collapsed facedown, and turned him over. He was unresponsive, breathing shallowly. One eyeball was shot full of blood, his forehead split open so that we could see layers of flesh and muscle, like an anatomical rendering. I settled down to check vitals and give what emergency care I could as Cal called for medical attention. Field response—coming back from my time overseas as though it had never been away.

Turned out the driver, Ted Dunston, was 19 years old. Drivers license from Maine, and he was registered in college there, but no family to be found. What he was doing in our part of the world no one knew. Nor did we ever find out what caused the collision. Why he was driving 65 mph down Walnut, why he stumbled away afterward. And a Lincoln Town Car? Hardly a typical choice for someone his age. But it was his, bought used almost a year back. By the time they did blood work and tox screens, once he'd been stabilized at the local hospital and shipped up to University Hospital three hours away, the tests didn't have much to tell. No evidence of drugs. No discernible sign of physical impairment or injury other than damage sustained in the crash.

He was put on a ventilator, died a year and a half later of pneumonia.

"Yeah, it happens here, too," Cal said the day of the crash, "just like it does in jungles and deserts. Try to find a reason for it, an explanation, you'll just make yourself half crazy, everyone around you too."

By this time Cal had learned more about my background than anyone else would ever know, except for Sid, years later. As I said, this was six days in, the two of us sitting day after day going over procedure, legal issues, talk-down techniques, investigation routines, department guidelines. We'd break every couple of hours and head to Mindy's for coffee and less formal conversation. I never learned much about Cal but I did learn a lot of basic law that week and the next three, after which I was on my own, working 4 to 12 most days, swinging to nights when for whatever reason we needed full coverage, or else taking call. Cal told me state scholarships were available to peace officers who wanted to attend law school part-time, working around their schedules, and suggested that I think about it. When I asked him if he was serious—college again at my age?—he said I'd be bringing experiences into the classroom, a world really, that most others would never see.

I was remembering that crash as I worked a collision out by the highway. A well-battered pickup with three workers in the back on their way to a construction site and a sub-compact driven by a night-shift worker on her way home had aimed for the same spot in the left lane, just past seven in the morning. No one was hurt, just badly shaken up, but there was considerable damage to the car, and the truck now had a few new war wounds.

I diagrammed the collision, waited for the wrecker to

come get the car, dropped the car's driver off at her home, went back to the office to complete paperwork and transcribe what everyone at the scene had said while it was still fresh. Not required and not standard practice, but it was a habit I'd gotten into, more for my own use than for any other reason, to boost recall should the need arise.

I was coming back from lunch. He was sitting on the bench outside City Hall, on the pew salvaged from a community church built around the same time as the town, that had mostly fallen back to earth on its own before getting torn down. He looked as though he hadn't a care in the world and could barely imagine that others might. Dark blue, lightweight suit of a kind that doesn't much wrinkle, white shirt, medium-gray tie. Good shoes. A light-skinned black man with high cheekbones, crow-black straight hair. Frequent flyer at his barber's.

"You're Sheriff Pullman."

"And you're yet another in the throng of tourists come to sample our town's attractions?"

"Well, it *is* a nice bench. Though I do miss having the cardboard fan with Bible verses tucked into the pew ahead of me."

Which probably set his age north of fifty and, despite the lack of accent, suggested a rural upbringing.

"I'm afraid church has let out."

"All about the country, it would seem." He stood and held out his hand. "Tyrell Martin."

"Care for coffee?"

"Every time. Still plenty of that around, thankfully."

We went in and, as I suspected, Brag, knowing my habits, had brewed a fresh pot while I was gone. My visitor said black when I held up the mug to ask. We sat in the padded chairs by the window. Never much cared for sitting at the desk. Still thought of it as Cal's, in a way.

"Government?" I said.

"Special agent, FBI." He'd crossed his legs and leaned back into the chair.

"The FBI comes to Farr."

"Lions and tigers, oh my."

"And not simply passing through."

He sipped coffee, nodded approval. "Settling into the job okay?"

"Doing my best to."

"Had to have caught you unprepared."

"Like this conversation."

"On the other hand, you do have the background for it."

"And just how is it you came to know my background?"

"I rarely leave the office without a full briefing. You never know what may be out on the edges, where the lines fall. And we have a roomful of people hunched over computers just waiting for the spark that gets fingers moving."

He smiled. I smiled. Two beacons of the social order sitting together politely, talking over how things are.

I had to wonder what those fingers had found, what he knew. But he leaned away from that.

"Calvin Phillips," he said. "I don't suppose you've heard from him, or had any word?"

"This is an official question?"

"A curious one. Flags came up when your bulletins about him hit."

"Then I'll trade curiosities with you. Why the interest in a small-town sheriff?"

"I can't say more."

"If that's the level of cooperation we have, you should give me back my coffee."

"Too late, I'm afraid." He set the empty mug on the windowsill. "Not a huge fan of authority are you, Sheriff?"

"Or of bullshit."

"Yet here you are. In authority yourself." He stood. "I'll be around. If something turns up—"

"If it does, I expect you'll know it."

"I'm thinking something not out there for the world at large, something more personal."

Within an hour of Agent Martin leaving, I got called out to the high school, where fourteen students were "disrupting classes" in their protest of new dress codes. The only disruption I could see consisted of their being absent from classes; they were standing quietly in a line in the hallway outside the principal's office holding neatly stenciled signs. Ordinarily, and without difficulty, the protest would have been shut down and the protestors sent home, but one of the students was the school's top football player and the best musician in the band, and another was the daughter of the town's premiere physician, a surgeon who'd made the decision to leave big-city, high-profile life for a more easeful one in Farr.

Principal Giblin was unsure what he expected me to do when I asked. He'd been in the position less than six months following the previous principal's retirement.

"It's purely an internal problem," I told him. "There's no threat, implied or otherwise, to the community, others, or themselves. Besides which, students do have the right to assemble."

"Not on school property. And not on school time."

"That could be argued. And while it lies within your purview to dismiss or discipline them, you haven't done so."

"I didn't want to make this any worse than it is, to make more of it."

"And you thought calling us in would avoid that?"

We'd been talking in the office, his eyes repeatedly coming back to meet mine before being drawn again to the half-glass of the door and hallway beyond. I had to wonder if he was mugwumpish like this at home, wherever home was, whoever was in it.

There are three possible responses to peaceful demonstration, I told him. Ignore it, call out the palace guards, or open a dialogue. He decided on the last, spoke with the protestors, and set a meeting for late that week, open to all students and parents, to discuss the issue and (his words) put it to rest. The fuss was over wearing hoodies or T-shirts with slogans, band imagery, brand names and the like. On the one hand, it did seem silly: This, of all the world's wrongs, merited protest? On the other, finding some balance between group identification and individuation is how we mature, isn't it? As self, and as a society.

11.

Few days go by that I don't think about my mother disappearing on us then turning back up days or weeks later as though she'd never left, along with the thought that I'd taken after her, except for the showing up again.

Or how Daddy wrote me letters those last couple of years when he'd moved into the trailer. I don't think he'd ever written a letter before in his life. And there I was, getting one every month or two. I rarely left a forwarding address, but somehow his letters, some of them anyway, found their way to me. Got the first one when I stopped by to see an old landlady I'd grown close to. She'd held on to it going on three months just in case I came by.

Pretty,
Your mom came home. Sounds like the start of a tall tale or the punch line of a joke when I write it down like that, don't it? She says it's for good this time. But we know better.

I'm sitting at what passes for a kitchen table here in the trailer, a slab of formica screwed to the wall on one side with a couple of pitiful legs on the other. The lights are flickering again.

It's damn peculiar to write this knowing all odds are against you ever seeing it. I'd tell you the news but there isn't any, we all just go on like we always have, sinking slowly into the ground.

Speaking of which, I do go back over to the house once in a while to look and see is there anything I can do to shore it up. There's wood could be salvaged, but I just can't find energy or reason.

Wherever you are, Pretty, I hope you're doing well. Your old man misses you. Not sure if you know this, but I always thought you'd be the one who'd manage to get out of all this. Was I right?

That's how most of the letters read, same length, same pattern, same words more or less. They'd stagger in, exhausted from banging about from place to place, and claim squatter's rights on the refrigerator, countertop, kitchen table or desk drawer. As time went on, they resembled one another more and more, like boilerplate wills or divorce papers you pull off the internet to fill in blanks, until, finally, new letters were virtual copies of older ones.

Then this:

Sarah Jane,

I know Shell's been in touch, or he's attempted to be. Whether he succeeded, I don't know. If he did, maybe he mentioned that we'd been together again. But whichever's true, I've left and won't be back. He's been living in a trailer for years now. Again, you may know this. The house is little more than a pile of lumber and rubble and drywall. When he moved to the trailer, it was like his world shrank to fit, like the world got to be the size of that trailer and what little he was able to see from in there, and it's gone on shrinking, getting smaller and smaller every day since. How can he breathe? He doesn't go out. The blinds are pulled shut all the time. A little TV on the counter of the so-called galley is always on. For company, he says. Last week it went wonky and nothing would play but static. I don't think he noticed until I asked him about it. So I'm still here, just across town, but one foot's somewhere else, I'm leaning into the wind, and the wind's blowing hard. Love always.

Six weeks after that letter came, Brag and I are driving up to Grove with a prisoner we're delivering on an outstanding felony warrant, talking about nothing in particular till he says, "KC told me you got a call from Cal."

"I did."

"And that he'd been by your place."

"Maybe it was him."

"Just the one call?"

"And a short one. He wanted to know how I was doing, how the town was getting along."

"That's Cal all right. And that?" He points: a two-year-old F-150 pulled to roadside, its driver, a middle-aged woman, waving us down. "That FBI guy ever tell you more about what he wanted?"

"Agent Tyrell Martin. No."

We pull in behind. The truck cut out on her without warning, she says—fuel pump maybe? With the prisoner aboard we can't give her a ride, but we radio back to town and have the garage send out a truck, then wait with her.

Once we're back on the road, Brag picks up where he left off. "Cal didn't let on to anything? When he called?"

"Only that when he first came home he'd been messed up, did things he regretted."

"PTSD. Damaged goods."

"Could be. I stay suspicious of acronyms, catch phrases, slogans. We use them, they make us think we understand. But they *keep* us from understanding. From looking closer."

Our passenger, who hasn't spoken since we left town but evidently has been listening, leans forward in the back seat. "Don't have to be a soldier to have damage. All got our share."

Brag turns to him. "Damn right."

"Like most everything else," I say, "the question's where it takes you."

"Ain't much doubt where it's taken *me*," our passenger says.

One time when Mother was home and I was maybe seven or eight, before the bedrooms got shifted around and about the time I started writing things down, I could hear them through the wall at night. She was talking about where she'd been before she showed up again, some special place, she kept saying, and some experience she'd had there, how she'd come to understand . . . (I couldn't make out the rest.) What I remember most is the last part, after Daddy told her she was talking nonsense, and the truth was, and so on.

"It's not that simple, Shell."

"It's not that complicated either. Not unless you make it—and then there's no end to the thing, it'll go on and on for as long as you stretch it."

A few days after this, I heard one of Daddy's friends use the term *duck blind*. I didn't know what a duck blind was, but I loved the sound of the words, those two blunt syllables, and marched around for days saying them over and over. Later I'd come to admire how the words functioned ambiguously as noun, verb or descriptive adjective, all the possible, strange meanings swimming around underneath.

Why do I connect those two fragments of overheard conversation in my mind?

"What evil lurks in the hearts of men?" *The Shadow*'s announcer always declaimed.

And what unspoken understandings?

12.

Farr was in the throes of a street festival. Crowds by the half-dozen filled downtown, squeezing in and out of shops, lining up at Bo's taco stand or Annabell's Treasure Booth while the high school band gallantly and mostly on key if not quite in time played a mix of century-old sentimental songs and show tunes maybe half that age. Kids from the Lutheran Church were putting on a gymnastics show in the bare corner lot where the old Landmark Bank had been torn down. Calling that lot our city park had begun as a joke and caught on.

The town library was there in the person of Miss Bly, a twentyish woman who seemed composed entirely of freckles and excitement. Odie Simon had his watches on display. He'd been collecting them all his life. Pocket watches from the last century, diver's watches, a Cartier, one German-made with as many switches and pulls as an aircraft cockpit, Japanese designs that looked liquid and almost alive. Jimmy Dolan played guitar and sang country music at one makeshift booth, with a stack of CDs, *Lonely Way Home*, on the table by him.

I grabbed to-go coffee at the diner and made the rounds. Anywhere you looked, pleasantries sat up on hind legs pawing at the air. To a man, to a woman, all the people of Farr had gone happy and cheerful. Truth to tell, it was kind of scary, like that moment in the movie with bright music and smiles, before the monster lurches onstage, before the distant sound of cannons.

Laura Chen motioned me over to her booth to show me the latest, a vast selection of earrings, bracelets and necklaces made of antique silverware.

"I know you don't wear jewelry, Sarah, but isn't this beautiful?"

I had to admit it was. Many pieces were silver, some with dark tarnish that could no longer be rubbed away, the edges of some of the spoons worn paper thin.

"By the way, did your old friend find you?"

"Sorry?"

"Yesterday or the day before. Good looking fella? Said he was passing through, thought to look you up."

Not yet, I told her, and asked for a description before stepping away. What I got wasn't much to go on, but I had my suspicions. I put on a smile to match those around me, strolled, and sipped my coffee.

Okay. So now I had some guy poking around the house,

a supposed old friend asking after me, phone calls that might as well be from a ghost. How did any of this make sense?

I went back to the office, sat in Cal's wooden swivel chair that had gashes and scrapes everywhere, was missing most of one arm, and groaned whenever I shifted weight. Out my window the festival continued silently. Phones rang in the front office a few times and I could hear Andrea talking, but I couldn't make out any of it and no one transferred a call or came in.

Later that day, in what passes for rush-hour traffic in Farr, we had a major pile-up on Cedar Wash Road, two cars and a pickup, complete with standard-issue declarations of came out of nowhere, couldn't stop in time. No one was hurt and none of the vehicles were severely damaged, but one car had to be towed, and insurance companies would keep busy playing feint and dodge for a while.

Afternoon also brought a visit from frequent flyer Mrs. Danzig, fifty-six going on eighty. Believing it memory, Mrs. Danzig toted around within her an indelible imprint of the world as it should be, and passed her time trying to fit the world she saw about her to that image. When she needed relief, she came in to see me. She spoke. I listened. In towns like Farr, law officers serve as confessors the same way priests and pastors do.

The latest glitch in programming was the lady lawyer who'd moved in next door after the Finlays packed up and moved to Florida or Louisiana or one of those places that had alligators roaming the streets. Cindy her name was, looked too young to be a lawyer but claimed she was, didn't do a thing to take care of the house or fit into the neighborhood. Rarely put out her trash barrels for pickup, let the lawn grow for weeks at a time, mail piled up in the box by the front door till it spilled out. What it seemed like was she didn't even live there, she lived somewhere else and every few days came round, stayed a night or two, then was gone again. Meanwhile, there or not, most of the time her car sat in the driveway pulled up to a small junky trailer, and parked on the street out front was some brokedown piece of a car that was as much an eyesore as the trailer.

I told Mrs. Danzig I'd look into it. She thanked me, held out a hand smelling of lavender to shake mine, and shuttled out the door, her gait a blend of arthritic pain and the grace (womanly, she'd call it) she had learned from her mother as a child.

As it turned out, I didn't get around to following up on Mrs. Danzig's complaint till the next morning. I ran the neighbor's license and tags, checked court records, put in a quick call to the state bar association. Cindy Brolin was proprietor and sole attorney at a law practice two towns over, in an old industrial center whose tire and chemical plants had shut down better than forty years ago, leaving the town with acres of deserted buildings and few jobs, the mean age of its population ever increasing as the young fled. Miss Brolin had attended the state university law school. Her specialty was criminal law but she'd drifted into property law and estate planning. In recent years the records showed her doing public defender work; in recent months, not much of that.

I was twelve when the voices stopped. I had assumed everyone heard them, but the looks that came my way when I mentioned them caused me to shut that part of myself away from others. I kept quiet about the voices for years. Then they were gone.

Makes you think of imaginary playmates, guys wearing aluminum foil hats, blurry horror films, that kind of thing, right?

But it wasn't that kind of thing.

I heard them clearly, as though the speaker stood close beside me. Some of what they said didn't make any sense at all at first, some cleared up a bit as events took place in my life, some never did. I'm pretty sure now that this was my subconscious sending signals before it established more traditional channels, regular trade routes, so to speak, but at the time what I heard was as real as the ground underfoot.

And that, the night following the street festival, was

the night I thought the voices had returned. I woke—2:46, when I looked—with them rolling about my head, pillow case damp with sweat.

Images and words were evaporating as I woke, gone even as I reached for them. The emptiness they left behind tugged at my breath and heartbeat. Something about chickens, a newborn baby that couldn't cry, people living, generation after generation, in abandoned cars.

Only a dream.

I got up and stood at the window. The southern live oak out there was the most asymmetrical, misshapen tree I'd ever seen. It kept losing branches and limbs and patches of its trunk to insects, mold and fungus, to at least one car that crashed into it and, for all we know, to poor diet, gambling and the sins of its parents, but it refused to quit. People claimed that years and years ago some superstar gardener came to visit and said the tree had to be at least five hundred years old, said they could live to be a thousand.

Earlier that evening we'd got a call to Paul Manning's. His neighbor had gone out to feed her nightly pack of feral cats and heard sounds, raised voices, from the Manning house. Looking over what remained of the common wooden fence, she saw two men shouting at Paul, who stood on his back porch with head bowed. They were gone when I got there, but Paul still stood on the porch, as though he expected them back any moment.

"You have to feel sorry for the boy," Mabel Price said

when I went over to thank her for calling and to let her know that I'd got Paul settled in. "Nobody should have to . . ."

No, I agreed. No one should.

She, I knew from others in the office, mostly left him to his privacy but trod around to his front door once or twice a week with a fresh-baked casserole. We got calls almost as often.

Seven years back, responding to a report of possible gunfire, police found Paul's father and mother shot dead in their bed, the younger sister smothered in hers, and ten-year-old Paul to every appearance sleeping soundly. The sister's favorite doll was tucked into her arms.

This had happened one hot summer night, people recalled, when local news was filled to the brim with excitement about plans for the town's first, four-store strip mall and local gossip was all about Bobby Wattel, who'd started life in a storm-battered shack on the edge of town and was about to take his seat in the state legislature.

Paul, it turned out, was not simply sleeping. The police couldn't wake him, nor could doctors at the local hospital, nor those at the university hospital in the capitol. Diagnosed with coma of unknown origin, he was placed in a long-term care facility where, months later, having been until that time wholly unresponsive, one night he was found walking in the halls. He was, he said, looking for his sister. Had anyone seen her?

The only thing he could remember from the night of the murders was picking his sister's doll up from the floor and putting it in her arms.

Paul passed from the care facility to a juvenile rehab center, then to a series of foster homes. Somewhere in there, at one hearing or another, a family-court judge named Jerry Butler took an interest in the boy, followed up on his care, and eventually shepherded him through petitioning the courts for release from the system and a claim to what remained of the family estate, which wasn't much but enough to allow purchase of his small home. He worked as janitor at the junior high, coming in for work at day's end when most everyone was gone. The kids, when they were around, left him alone. Others, unable to forget the blood found on Paul, his bed and the sister's doll, didn't. Either they believed a ten-year-old had shot both parents and smothered his sister, or they were taking their cues from something more primal.

I swung back by the office after the call to Paul's. Brag was there, hanging up the phone with a final *Yes ma'am* and looking a bit disconnected himself. I asked if he was okay.

"Pastor Hamilton's wife, claiming she hears strange sounds from the church again. Said I'd send someone right out."

Most of the time, saying that was all it took. She'd move on to something else.

"Oh—and I'm taking Emily's shift, Sarah. Hope you're good with that. Husband's in the hospital again."

"The cancer?"

"Says it's in his spine now."

"I'll get by there tomorrow, let him know we're thinking of him."

I'd barely dropped into Cal's chair behind the desk when Brag came to the door.

"Paul okay?"

"Relatively. Second verse, same as the first."

He lingered.

"I'm a decent person, right, Sarah?"

Why do people do that? Because I'm older? A woman? Because I'm from the big world outside Farr? As someone to ask advice about how to live, I'm a damnably poor choice.

I nodded.

"So is Paul Manning. While you were out on call, I was thinking about him. He's never had much of a chance, has he?"

"Not really, but he gets along. Most people are kind to him. We chink up the cracks however we can."

The phone rang out front. A garbage truck humped its slow way down the alley behind.

"Like so much else, I guess. You just need to pull back and look. Thanks, Sarah."

I didn't add that empathy, the ability to put ourselves

into someone else's life however different that life may seem, is what will save us, if anything can.

And I didn't know then that Brag had been born to parents identified as severely retarded, who'd met in a special care facility where they'd been raised. Coming of age, they had petitioned for release, got married, and late in life gave birth to baby Brag—an intellectually normal child brought up in a home whose adults had limited cognitive skills and the barest understanding of emotions, motivations and relationships.

I learned that later.

And that, it turned out, was what would make him a great sheriff.

13.

And then there's this.

Having tread for years so lightly over minefields and eggshells, keeping to myself and feeling little draw toward the possibility of anything else, confident that I was done forever with such, I found myself again entangled with another human being.

Entangled. I sat here for most of an hour before setting down that word, the closest I can come to capturing at one and the same time what it felt like then and what it feels like now. Memory's a hunting horn but it only carries so far, and the game we're after is on to us, it keeps moving.

So, quite a long list, the taxonomy of romances. The Ever-so-civil Jane Austen, the Jane Eyre Attic Horror, the Sexless and Proper Henry James, the Barbara Cartland Standard. Trouble is, no one offers a menu. You take what the kitchen sends out.

We met when his Mercedes broke down and, cruising

outside town because nothing was going on closer in and I'd had my daily fill of butt and chair, I stopped to check on him. A Mercedes. Around Farr, that was like coming across someone riding a camel.

He had the hood up, and was sitting on the trunk. I called in the plate and approached, asking if he needed help. He had on jeans and a yellow polo. A sportcoat hung over the driver's seat. Hair was long and he hadn't shaved for a couple of days.

"Good chance of it."

"Stopped on you?"

He nodded.

"No sign of overheating, unusual noises, bumps or grinds?"

"I pulled over to answer a text and shut down the engine. Give her a rest, I thought. Then when I tried to start her back up, she wouldn't."

"This is an older model, right?"

"Almost twenty years. No way I could afford it otherwise."

He'd handed over license and registration without being asked, and I checked them.

"You're from Dunlap?" Suburb of the capitol, sixty-some miles upstream.

"Mostly."

"Have a regular mechanic up that way?"

"Did. Last year, he stopped too. A massive stroke. Mercy and I've been running on a wing and a prayer since."

"Mercy?"

"The car."

"You always name inanimate objects?"

"She wasn't inanimate up till an hour ago. By strict definition."

"Strict, slack or anywhere in between, you're screwed."

"Until you happened along."

"Good to be appreciated. Anything you need from the car?"

He shook his head.

"Best mechanic around here's Sonny Mayhall. Garage is attached to the Chevrolet dealer, but he does his own work out of there as well. Be happy to drop you off. If anyone can get you up and running quick and easy, Sonny can."

"That would be great. Thanks, Officer . . ."

"Sheriff. Sarah Pullman."

"A pleasure."

He held out his hand. The grip firm. At some point not too long ago, and for no inconsiderable time, those hands knew hard work.

We rode back into town—in off the prairie, my passenger said. At Sonny's he thanked me again and added, "C.D. McLendon. As you know from my license."

"Well, you did hand it over like you were trying to get rid of it."

"Mostly I go by Sid."

"The car has a nickname, you have to have one too?"

"Some things from our childhood won't go away. I did manage to shift it from Seedy to Sid."

"Definitely an upgrade."

"Even that took years."

Outside the Chevy showroom next door, with its expanse of tile, spotless windows and gleaming display models, a man had paused for a moment before walking in, woman and early-teens girl four or five steps behind him. The women were left to open the door for themselves. Everyone wore sturdy, well-used, well-kept clothes. Now, as the man and woman sat talking to a salesman, the girl stood inside by the front window and, looking around to see no one was watching, leaned forward to rub her nose against the sparkly clean glass. Leaving her mark.

Two days after that, I'm at the desk with my head down staring at budget columns and squiggles that might as well be cuneiform. Times like this, I give serious consideration to shutting off the lights, getting in my car, and seeing how the rear view mirror functions two or three states over. It's not my car, though, and sooner or later I'd have to bring it back.

"Sheriff?"

A voice from the great, wide world.

An envoy come from afar.

A lost tourist.

Sid McLendon.

"Mercy break down again?"

"Not yet." He came on into the room. Dark gray slacks, a seersucker sportcoat the like of which I hadn't seen since New Orleans, flaps tucked into side pockets. "Jury's still out as to the wing, but so far the prayer's holding. And your friend Sonny's ministrations. Still don't understand what it was he did that took all of four minutes."

"Back home they'd call it a laying-on of hands. But cars, people—some just don't go down easy."

"True." He'd been looking around the office as we spoke. Orderly shelves, decades-old filing cabinet with drawers seriously off plumb, bare plain of desk, two straight chairs by the window. "Minimally inclined, I see."

"We need about a tenth of what we think we do."

"Or less. Might you need lunch? I'm down this way on business, thought buying you lunch would be a proper thank-you."

"And your business is?"

"Honestly I don't often own up to it, and pass myself off as a salesman, an accountant. Staves off a ton of worthless conversation."

He pointed to one of the chairs for permission and, when I nodded, soundlessly lifted it, placed it before the desk, and sat.

"I'm a lawyer. Court-appointed, social-support organizations, non-profits."

"In it for the big money, then."

"I *do* drive a Mercedes, you know."

Over lunch, as side dishes with my club sandwich and his grilled cheese, we had healthy portions of here-I-am from Sid and myself. Where we came from. How we got here. What we did in between.

We'd moved on to coffee when he said, "Maybe you left something out?"

"Should I have spoken faster? Eaten slower?"

"The other day, when you stopped. You approached with the sun behind you."

"You were facing west."

"And you U-turned to come in how you did."

"Okay."

"That, and the way you approached, looked a lot like military training."

So I told him. Not the heavy stuff, that came later, but the dailyness, the shape of it. Desert, heat, smells, getting hit by the RPG. Not about Oscar. That would happen months along, halfway through a night, with car tires ripping water off rain-drenched streets outside and the glow of a night light from the next room, Sid sitting dead still with his hand on mine.

As for Sid, he'd had (he said) one of those storybook childhoods you think never really existed: ranging freely through the neighborhood, doors of the home left unlocked, no worries as he, sister and friends biked to the city playground or library, spent summer afternoons unsupervised at the swimming pool, drank Pepsi and Dr Pepper from the cooler at the service station up the street, checked out goods at the army surplus store, rambled through the junkyard just outside the city limits, bought comics at Riley's Drugstore that still had the soda fountain from the forties when it was built. His world, he admitted, had been a bubble in time, or more accurately, out of time. A lost world.

Then he went off to school, on scholarship which was the only way he'd have been able to, and everything changed. Food, attitudes, accents, clothing, ways of thinking—he'd had no idea such variety existed. No idea that people could own so many things or believe so many things and despise those who didn't.

Freshman year, he'd had a great American history professor, which first gave him over to thoughts of a political life. But as he made his way more deeply into that history, with his own experience alongside as template, he understood how governance dragged behind it a relentless desire for ever more control, and for self-preservation. What was needed wasn't more governance but protection from its excesses. Safeguards. Nay-sayers. Civil disobedience. Legal challenges.

His partner at the time sided with Spengler: All cultures begin as cults, with spiritual exercises meant to channel the struggle for survival into a supposed pursuit of ideals. But then, as the culture ages, its institutions take over, replacing the idealism that first fueled it.

"Such was the heady soup I lived in," Sid said. "Salvation. Damnation. Redemption."

"Big words."

"That never make us happy. But I survived the heady soup, the break-up, even my own dreary seriousness."

"Tough man."

"Stubborn can get you a long way."

As for the military, he hadn't served but he represented many who did. The damaged, maimed, discarded, cancer-stricken, indelibly scarred. Pieces of them carved away, thrown away, by promises no one intended to keep.

"Think we should get back to work?" Sid said with our third refill. He'd nestled his empty shot containers of half-and-half inside one another, six of them. "Maintain the social contract. Uphold community standards. Stir the pot."

He stood to carry plates, utensils and detritus to the place provided at the counter's far end.

"The pot's still there on the back of the stove, over a fire so low sometimes you think it's gone out. We've been throwing in scraps for two hundred and fifty years."

14.

I was looking over a memo and attachments, thinking how best I could get off that chair, out of there, and into sunlight, looking forward to an early dinner with Sid, when the first calls came in. The memo said I was supposed to be evaluating employees. The attachments offered helpful suggestions and guidelines. Sure thing, get right on it. Better yet, let's evaluate the city council members who'd reached up and plucked this idiocy out of thin air.

Initial thoughts, when the calls started? Mormons, Seventh Day Adventists, Christian Scientists. Proselytizers of some manner. Eight to ten young people, male and female, twentyish, making their way door to door downtown. All of them plainly dressed, dark trousers or skirts, white shirts or light blue tops, ties on the men, simple accessories for the women. Even with the group's being steadfastly polite, apologizing for the intrusion, asking if they might have a moment, withdrawing immediately upon request, some businesses and townfolk were uneasy with this.

Fifth phone call, I decided to go have a look.

One of the women was exiting Fox Flower as I approached to introduce myself. She pulled out her driver's license and student ID and handed it over as we spoke. Christine Sonnerson, junior at Owen College.

"I'm sorry, Sheriff, is a permit required? Forgive us if so. We weren't informed."

Nothing like that, I assured her, but this being out of the ordinary, concerns had been expressed. I returned her IDs. Would she mind telling me what she and her companions were doing here?

Not at all. They weren't soliciting, if that was the problem. Well, she supposed they were, actually, though they weren't selling anything.

Selling? Maybe not, but definitely peddling, and what these young people had in their cart was age-old conservativism dressed up in spiffy new clothes, wrapped about with civility and proper grammar.

"I have literature," Miss Sonnerson told me. "Our handler said we're to give it out only when it seemed welcome."

I leafed through the brochure she offered. Six pages, tastefully designed, expertly produced. Amazing what technology makes possible these days. Quite a step up from the photocopies and back-room print jobs of my youth, and not only in production. The writing was solid as well, pinned throughout with sidebars from movement participants.

I was 12 when I realized the world described to me was quite different from the one I saw. And different from another I could imagine. It seemed that not only did I have a choice, I had those three choices.

—

The desire of the individual for freedom and society's need for controls are forever in contest. Who wins in the struggle? No one. But the struggle itself is central—both to government, and to how we live our lives.

—

Don't say will not, say why not.

We only hope to be heard, Miss Sonnerson said. And to that end, we speak softly.

I thanked her for her time and asked her to carry on, adding, just before she stepped away, "You do understand that male supremacy's a part of the package? You must."

"Of course. But packages can be readdressed. Put inside bigger boxes."

Her group spent the afternoon in town, gaining precious

little interest or support, I suspect, but causing no real problem, and left in early evening as dark began to claim footholds. The next I'd hear of Ms. Sonnerson was years later, as she prepared to take a seat in the state Senate.

The worst of it can come not in the dark as you'd expect, but in early light, when at 5 or 5:15 you wake with the world piecing itself back together outside and pieces of your life rattling about in your head like loose teeth in a cup.

As things turned out, I hadn't made it to dinner last night. Sid said no problem, he understood, when I called. The call was two hours late. A fight at Maggie's just outside the city limits, with a man no one knew insisting upon cutting in for a dance, had somehow escalated to a free-for-all. Maggie's son Chill called it in. I was still at the office, went right out there, and ended up rousing Brag from home to help sort it.

We took statements, told Chill how much we'd hate to have to shut the bar down if this were to happen again, listened politely to his protestations of innocence, advised half a dozen patrons to go to ER to get checked out. One, who almost certainly had a broken arm, Brag drove to the hospital himself.

I called Sid to apologize and beg off dinner. Lunch tomorrow, maybe? Or breakfast? Went home, cobbled up a grilled cheese from suspicious fragments unearthed in the refrigerator, added a sliced apple. Cinnamon tea doubled as beverage and dessert.

Then woke at early light with a sore throat, gritty eyes, and a headful of half-remembered images from dreams. I made French press coffee and went out on the porch.

The yellow-orange cat from down the street walked by with a bird in her mouth, a dove, I think. Every few minutes she'd put it down and cry out. The kittens she birthed eight or nine weeks ago now had new homes. She still went through the neighborhood looking for them, crying out, with dead birds she'd brought to feed them and teach them about being cats.

However hard we try, we know so little about what goes on in anyone else's head. Far less a cat's. Did she simply feel the loss, an emptiness? Did she know it for what it was? How much could she understand of what happened? How much do any of us?

By eight I'd finished the coffee, watched as the mother cat carried the dove back the way she came, showered, found clean clothes, found sufficient wherewithal to get my butt to work.

The wherewithal I'd summoned to get me to the office wasn't sufficient to keep me there. By mid-morning I was out the back door and headed north.

I'd got in the habit of cruising Cal's place every few days.

Swing by, maybe stop and rest a bit, look around. What you try to do is see it all as a whole. You're not thinking, just looking, taking it in. Maybe something seems misplaced or doesn't fit, something not quite right out along the edge, or there by that entryway. Pattern recognition.

So I was sitting off a bit from the house, in a stand of pecan trees, drinking industrial-size and -strength coffee I'd picked up on my way out of town and thinking about nothing in particular, really worrying at it.

But something . . .

I flipped back through what I'd seen, focusing now. Wasn't near the house itself, the driveway, the road leading in. To the right. A slight movement in the trees beyond—which could, for all I knew, be wildlife.

Slipping from the car, I took to the trees to my left, moved as silently as possible in a long arc that would bring me in behind. As I drew close, an opening appeared in the trees and, at the very moment I entered, a man stepped in opposite me. He'd been carrying a shotgun, barrel broken, in the crook of his arm. Now he snapped it shut.

He wore a couple of plaid shirts that didn't come close to matching, one of them unbuttoned, with heavy grey work pants. A full head of dark hair wholly out of synch with the aged face beneath.

"Sarah Pullman," I said. "Acting sheriff."

"Thought it might be." The shotgun clicked back open. "Cal thought a lot of you."

"As I did of him."

"You up here for?"

"Been coming by now and again."

"Saw you." He posted the gun on his shoulder. "Cal's one bird who won't be coming back to the tree."

"You know that?"

"Much as I know anything."

"Yet you're here."

"Same's you. Asking myself why."

We walked through the trees, across a meadow and shallow pond, to another clearing a mile or more away, where he had a trailer. Started out as a hunter's shed back when this was wild land, he said, before the town reached out and grabbed at it. He'd tweaked the place some, built on a screen porch big as the trailer itself, hung another room on the back, painted the whole affair a dull flat brown, but remained off the grid. Power from a generator when needed, which wasn't often, water from a well. No telling what had soaked into the ground over the years, fertilizers and pesticides and the like, that he was drinking. But not much telling what the town *put* in, either.

His name was Maury but he went by Mole. He'd offer me a drink but what had been a good close companion for much of his life had turned on him some twenty years back. There was coffee to be had, if I had the notion.

Cal was another close companion?

Hard to say. Both were of a kind to keep their distance,

but they had common ground. Age laying the same claim on them as it was, growing up out in the country away from others. Fought in different wars but how different are they, you come right down to it? What I heard, Mole said, you know about that.

By that time the coffee was ready. He'd made it in a stove-burner percolator the like of which I hadn't seen outside of a junk store for decades. The trailer's entry door stood open. All the screened windows were open as well, one or two, from the look of them, permanently. A window fan moved air with all the force of a sigh.

Something'd been on Cal's mind this last couple months, not that he'd of spoken up. And it was not long after, that Mole started to wonder what might be going on over at Cal's place. Thought he caught movement over that way but when he got closer couldn't find anything. Some footprints that were out of place, since they weren't Cal's and Cal didn't have visitors. Sound of a truck or van once or twice. Like that.

"Nothing since Cal left," Mole said. I declined more of the stringent, metallic-tasting coffee as he poured himself a second cup. "Still keep an eye out. Two of us've known each other a long time."

"During your service?"

"Just after."

The largest raccoon I ever saw walked in the open door.

"Hold on," Mole said. "Short Girl's hungry."

He took a plate from a shelf by the sink, opened a plastic container and scooped out kibble. Put the plate down by the door.

"Used to bring the whole family around, quite a sight, but the little ones are gone now, I guess. She shows up regular, sometimes twice a day."

Short Girl, it turned out, was a delicate eater. We sat watching her pick a single piece from the plate, chew, go back for another. After a while I said, "Cal called me once when he'd been gone a while—just the one time. Said when he first got back home he'd been messed up. Did things he regretted."

"Lots of us came back with a load on, you know how that is. We never talked about it."

Short Girl finished her food and went thumping down the stairs, stopping for water at the galvanized pan outside before going back to her other, her real, life.

15.

Morning mists were still burning away when I found the body.

Cars sat in driveways and at curbside, homemade trailer outside the garage, just as Mrs. Danzig described. Drapes were drawn, mailbox hanging vertical by the single remaining screw and choked with mail. No response to the bell, which I heard ringing inside, or to vigorous knocks.

I went back to the car and got my crowbar out of the trunk. The door gave easily, bolt tearing its way out of soft wood with hardly a sound. Stepping inside, I heard music from deeper within, music that stopped me cold for a minute. It wasn't baroque, something soft and mildly jazzy instead, but music, the lock tearing out of the frame—everything began to feel like the day I'd walked into Mr. Patch's house and found him in the bathtub. Dead, like Cindy Brolin.

Mr. Patch had looked at peace. Miss Brolin didn't.

She had hanged herself in the bathroom, from a ceiling joist, with a length of bright yellow plastic rope. It had done its job, then over time stretched to the point that her feet dragged the floor beneath bent knees. As though she were kneeling. The footstool she had used lay on its side nearby. She'd been up there, I figured, three to four days, maybe more. There was no note I could find. A book of cartoons lay perfectly aligned on the back of the toilet. She had fresh red polish on her toenails.

I called it in to the office, went next door to tell Mrs. Danzig what had happened, then back to the house to wait for the ME and body pickup. There was little of a personal nature on Cindy Brolin's computer. Emails that looked to be mostly work related; hopscotch visits to commercial websites for women's clothing and collector's costume jewelry; legal case files, updates for which petered off and, as of two months ago, all but stopped.

The unreasonable silence of the world, as Dr. Balducci, by way of Camus, once said.

Images like that, Cindy Brolin's head and face, the bright yellow rope, how it stretched so that she was kneeling, they stay with you. You start to remember all the other deaths. You think of the cat you found in the back yard when you were five or six. Her body and legs were stiff, she was breathing faster than seemed possible, her eyes were oddly white and fixed straight ahead. She knew you were there, you could sense that, but she didn't respond. Did she understand what was happening? Was she fighting against death? Kneeling beside her and stroking her matted fur, you named her Missy. You told her it was okay, she could just let go, it was okay.

Mayor Baumann had taken a dislike to me for my correcting him on points of law. At some level, I was pretty sure, he was also pissed off that I hadn't found Cal and brought him back, in order to get rid of me if nothing else. It was Cal, naturally, to whom I owed much of the knowledge allowing me to correct the mayor.

At any rate, lunch with Will Baumann was never a free meal. You could ignore the glad-handing, his sidelong glances to see who might be looking on, interruptions from shoppers satisfied or displeased with furniture purchased at W. Baumann & Son. But a summons is a summons, be it to court or to a session of favor bartering.

Stu Coleman's development plans, championed by the mayor, had gone south shortly after I stepped in as acting sheriff, nixed by townfolk. Since then he'd given up what I thought to be flirtation but was never sure. Could be it was just another shape for what he was at heart, a salesman, same as his politics. Or simply another verse of the age-old whale song of the white American male.

Today, budget cuts joined our soup 'n' sandwich specials on the table. Revenues were declining, taxes rising, more than one business was steps away from nailing the doors shut, the school system stayed aloft on blind faith, the hospital was on economic life support.

And the sheriff's department, of course, had its part to sing in this chorus of belt tightening and dollar pinching. Austerity measures, as Europeans call them. Surely I understood.

I looked at him over my club sandwich and waited.

What it came down to, though it took most of my sandwich and soup to get there, was that I had to let one of my people go.

"Like Moses to the Pharoah."

"Come on, Sarah, help me out here. It's for the town."

"Will, I get paid half what a decent housepainter does. For that I'm called on to ride herd on the town's kids, settle marital disputes, monitor traffic, track down the occasional thief, plow my way into bar fights, confront all kinds of people hell bent on trouble. Not that I should get paid more—I'm an amateur, no question. And no one else in the department's adequately trained for what they're called on to do, either. The town's consistently refused to pay for that. But my people do it anyway. They pull down just over minimum wage. Their checks pay rent, buy a sack or two of groceries, cover most of the bills unless something happens, the car breaks down, maybe, or someone gets sick."

"We don't have the money, Sarah. It's that simple."

"Only if you're looking at it simply."

"Why does every conversation with you have to turn into an argument?"

"The town's not a furniture business, Will. Not just what comes in, what goes out. But look, I have a solution for you."

Mattie had brought us both coffee by this time. The mayor lined up three packets of sweetener, tore them open all at once, and dumped them in.

"Instead of a civics lesson?" he said.

"You need to trim one person from the department, right?"

"As I said."

"Then I'm gone, everyone else stays. Problem solved."

"What, take one for the team? You're some kind of half-baked hero now?" He looked up to wave off an elderly man (furniture patron? political petitioner?) approaching the table. "Jesus. Even for you, this is out there."

Mattie had brought the check with our coffee. The mayor picked it up, a bit more dramatically than warranted, and stood.

"Truth is, you're seriously *off*, Sarah. Always have been."

He was right, of course.

Even to the moment I said I had a solution, I had no idea I was going to say that about quitting. And when I did say it, immediately I felt sadness, a sense of loss, settle upon me. But I also felt relief.

Cal's poster was still up, and I sat swiveled around in his chair looking at it.

IN THE TIME YOU'VE BEEN DISCUSSING
THE LATEST CELEBRITY'S TUMMY TUCK
44 VETERANS HAVE COMMITTED SUICIDE

Cal's poster, Cal's chair, Cal's people, Cal's job. Mine now. We'd see.

Sometimes it's like you go on practicing for the performance day after day without ever getting to read a script or know what your part is. Or you're standing in the park with a map that says, in this big box with bold letters, YOU ARE HERE, and you know damn well you're not.

Cal's job. People's pain.

What you see and feel in others, ultimately, is what you're able to reach down and find in yourself.

The mayor had repeated his sentiments during a visit to the office later that afternoon ("I meant what I said about your being off, Sarah. You are. People sense it") while at the same time pledging no interference, personnel cuts or otherwise, with the department. Not long after he left, KC reminded me it was six years this month that Will's wife died in the traffic accident out on the loop, and that the store's W. Baumann & Son was pure wishfulness. Donnie had decamped for the charms, anonymity and distance of the city late that same year.

I sat thinking of the mayor's fixed smile and one-of-a-kind comb-over, how perfectly suited they would be to a ventriloquist's dummy.

So much for deep thoughts and empathy.

So much, too, for our efforts to curtail drag races out by the old Pentecostal Church, news of which—one vehicle totaled, another in a ditch, serious injuries—reached us by phone as KC and I were talking. That kept us busy through the rest of the afternoon, past evening cicada calls, to dark. Interviews, photos, sketches, measurements. Danny Bevilacque, who'd been driving the crash, had at least a broken shoulder and leg; the ambulance guys took spinal precautions. Bo Dooley'd been in the ditch but seemed okay aside from bruises on his chest and arms and a goose egg over his right eye.

Both boys insisted they weren't racing. Something went wrong with the accelerator, Danny said, it jammed, the cable broke, something. He'd finished a rebuild of the carburetor on his street car the day before and was out here trying it out when, coming into that long curve, he started picking up speed. Shifted down much as he could but—next thing he knew, he was halfway up a tree. Bo told us he'd driven his car into the ditch to get out of the way of Danny's. From the look of the scene, weird as the stories were, they were telling the truth.

I got home well after dark and was standing in the kitchen eating an apple gone soft with time and a slice of cheese that I remembered looking quite different upon purchase, when the refrigerator door, shingled as it was with restaurant menus, special-offer coupons, photos, an anonymous picture postcard from Minnesota, a letter or two I'd meant to answer, to-do lists long forgotten, and images torn from magazine pages, caught my eye.

Patterns. The whole of it, taken in all at a glance, looked the same as before. But as my eye passed over the door and its layers, my subconscious snagged on it, and upon inspection subtle misplacements seemed evident: an edge out of kilter, altered spacings, curled edges that hadn't been. A rate-increase note from the power company that I barely remembered had migrated to the top. Someone had been in here. Someone had gone through this, then put everything back just as it was. Almost as it was.

Who? And why *almost*?

16.

"What happens is, you get down toward the end and you hope your life, though you can't see this however hard a look you take, you hope your life had some shape to it. Not meaning or a purpose, that brand of bullcrap. Just that it had a shape, wasn't some glob of stuff slapped on a plate."

Abel Holland was eighty-two years old. Claiming "cognitive problems," multiple incidents of inappropriate behavior or speech, and general unfitness to care for himself, two of his children were trying to have him declared incompetent. The third disagreed and, as the disagreement escalated, I got called in.

Hard to say what was behind this. Usually it's money or possessions, sometimes no more than a power play. None seemed to apply in this case. Abel had few possessions and lived off Social Security. There was nothing to exercise power over—except, of course, one another. Nor did the two petitioners manifest much by way of emotional concern for their father. There's little that's uglier than such intra-family disputes.

What Abel was saying made perfect, plain sense to me. But it didn't to the two pressing hard for a judgment against their father. They never so much as stopped to think about what he was saying, simply took it as further evidence of Abel's instability. About all we could do (as Judge Islip and I discussed afterward) was counsel them on probable outcomes should their behavior continue. Once you've shut down communication and blocked out logic and common sense, there's nothing left to you but digging in harder.

At one point as Abel and I spoke, I called him sir and he started up laughing. Spent eighty-two years getting called by names, he said, boy, nigra, colored, ever kind of name, but *sir*, that's a first. Just you look round us. Here in this courthouse where people of every stamp get brought together. And here we sit, a woman lawman and an old black man, together. Now that's a shape, Miss Sheriff. That, I swear by everything I've seen in my life, that surely is a shape, yes it is.

Hours later I reiterated my conversation with Abel Holland as Sid and I sat outside at a pie-slice divot of town sidewalk a new coffee bar had appropriated. "It's not unusual," he said, "for cultures to believe that to name something is to call it into being, even to have power over it." Earlier, in a light-footed remark carrying hidden weight, he'd expressed wonder and joy at my being free for the evening. We'd both feigned not to notice.

"But right now," he said, draining his cup, "what I'm looking to name is some food."

"Definitely could do with power over that."

"Chinese sound good?"

"Whoa. Big spender."

"Your turn to pay."

"Then strike that last remark."

Jenni was at the table almost before we sat, carrying tea and a tray of tiny egg rolls, making her usual fuss over us. Hadn't seen us in so long, how goes keeping the streets safe and people honest, had we had a chance to get away for a spell, decompress, take some deep breaths? She'd recently returned from a trip to China with her grandfather, to the village he was born in, her first visit ever. She was still trying to decide what she thought and felt about all she'd seen.

The bowling alley back home had mirrors mounted to either side. You'd lift your ball, glance at the mirror on the right, and there you were. The one on the left would have the same image mixed with a reflection of what came from the right mirror, and the right in turn (at least in imagination) would reflect both, arm after arm lifting bowling ball after bowling ball.

That's what Thursday felt like.

A state-wide bulletin waited when I got in that morning. There'd been a string of robberies at convenience stores in the north part of the state. Two males, one white, one possibly Hispanic, both late twenties to early thirties. The darker-skinned man carried a gun, what sounded from descriptions to be a .22. Small sums gained each time, as one would expect, most of these stores, chain and mom-and-pop alike, having gone to dropboxes. No pattern to time of day the stores were hit. And no real violence, yet.

I pulled up a state map on the computer and located the sites. They formed a series of lazy z's trending southward, always off the highways, swinging between state roads and side roads. Not much more to be gleaned from this, but the course the two were on, such as it was, conceivably could bring them close to Farr. I made a note to alert everyone to add multiple drive-bys for Joe's QuikE, Grab-Go and others to their routine patrols.

Much of the rest of the morning was given over to quarrel, gritch, grieve and their many kin. Smashed shelves during a confrontation over price at Meyers Clothing, kids who should have been in school brought in for tagging, a storeowner demanding we arrest a homeless man hanging around downtown, a young woman with no identification who'd been going from car to car trying doors in the mall parking lot.

Then, late afternoon, it started raining and looked as though it would go on forever. Our windows became rivers. Outside, cars ploughed at 15 mph through water halfway up their tires. The roof leak we'd had outside the supply room ever since I'd been here turned from drips and plops to a steady thin stream. We began to field calls for impassable roads, abandoned vehicles, parents frantically seeking children, wellness checks on aged relatives. At three-thirty the back door swung open to the downpour and Brag, who'd gone home after his night shift, splashed in. We could have wrung enough water out of his clothes to fill a truck bed.

"Figured you could do with some extra help."

"All we can get," KC said.

Phones rang, one after another and at the same time, out in the front offices as well. City clerk, traffic division, records.

"Always be waiting for rainbows, don't we?" KC said between calls.

"For all we know, there's one out there now." Brag had changed to spare clothes he kept in his locker. The clothes looked drier. He still looked soaked through. "No way we'd see it."

Already on the phone again, KC nodded.

Convenience-store robberies, break-ins, tagging kids, homeless men and foraging women had lost whatever urgency they had.

The rain slacked off toward seven. Thanks in large part to the wrecker and driver from Bing's Garage and to Brag, who left phones behind to brave again the swamp outside, the streets were mostly clear by nine-thirty. We decided that, further emergencies excepted, we'd all done enough for the day, closed down the office, and redirected calls to myself and KC. Stars began to show one by one, surfacing through the cloud cover. A light wind followed. It smelled of decay and new growth.

Sid and I had planned to have dinner together that night. Finally home, I found his note.

Called the department and couldn't get through. Don't know when or if you'll make it out of there. If you do, there are curried vegetables and rice in the oven, just need a warmup. Call tomorrow?

Given the circumstance, I wasn't sure if the last sentence was meant as an entreaty to me or was asking permission. That's the wobbly, knock-kneed state of mind I was in. I ate the rice and vegetables cold as I stood listening to bugs fly against screens and skitter down them, sent Sid an email of apology and thanks, and fell into bed still dressed.

Friday there was cleanup from the storm to do, and people were hard at it, so there wasn't a lot else going on. I had cleanup of my own, reports, expense vouchers, overtime requests, but instead sat looking out the window at what was essentially a tiny bit of corner raggedly torn from a photo, wondering what one might deduce of the actual world from such a sampling. In a jail cell, for instance.

I'd roused myself sufficiently to get up and pour a cup of coffee and was reclaiming my seat when a man walked by across the street. Within moments I was at the window. Solid build, with a low center of gravity and an easy gait that belied both. Nondescript brown hair gone shaggy, dark slacks, oversize white dress shirt with sleeves rolled. I was on my way out the door when Andrea, from the phone, signaled for me to wait. I was needed immediately, urgently, at Jewel's GasPlus.

KC, out on patrol, beat me there. He had one guy, head bloody, cuffed to the beer locker by the counter. The attendant had his right foot on the other one's arm and his left on the guy's neck. The restrained wrist had a huge gash with bone protruding.

KC held up a .22, pointing to the cuffed one.

"This criminal mastermind went back to the milk and dairy cooler. Hard to see from up here at the register. You have to crane your neck to look in the mirror by the ceiling, probably what they counted on. His buddy there came directly up to the counter. Mr. Tabrizi noticed they'd left the motor running."

I'd shut it down and grabbed the keys on my way in. Two teenagers had been hanging close by. No joy ride today.

"The one at the counter had the gun. Mr. Tabrizi

settled with him first. Blockhead saw that, tried to run, and fell, so he was next, while his bud was squirming on the floor."

Mr. Tabrizi handed me a baton. Well worn, grip rubbed smooth. Warm to the touch.

"In my country I was for eleven years a soldier," he said. "I will be under arrest now?"

"You will not." Holding up the baton, I told him I'd have to keep it a short while but would be certain it got safely back to him. He nodded, understandably still wary. In his country the ground could drop away beneath one's feet between heartbeats.

More paperwork, then. Arrest reports, prisoner login, personal item inventory. And a flagged bulletin to law enforcement agencies to inform all that we had in custody those we believed to be the convenience-store robbers. State authorities could come collect them at will.

Two days, straight up. Thursday's like making your way through a crowded bus that's bottoming out on every pothole in town. Friday, you're sitting in Cal's chair wondering what the hell someone who looks just like Pryor Mills is doing in Farr, walking down the street across from your office.

The name Pryor derives from the title given the head of a priory, of any religious collective, a monastery, an abbey, a nunnery. He's an official lower in rank than an abbot. I looked it up back when he and Bullhead started hanging together because I hadn't encountered the name before and had for the man who bore it an instinctive dislike that with time gave way to fear. Pryor was a fellow cop, Bullhead's main wingman. Before that he'd been some sort of marshall or deputy; details were vague in the same way that explanations for his departure from that previous position were. You'd probably want to start the list with insubordination, excessive use of force, misogyny, and brutality.

Some people make you uneasy, never meet your eyes. Once this man's eyes locked on, they never turned away. Stories about him sifted in from fellow cops, folks on the street, ER nurses, high school kids, hardline gamblers. It was a simpler time back then for some, a world drawn with edges clearly defined. White males hadn't been told or so much as imagined that they weren't privileged by birthright. Power was power. To keep it, you used it. And Mills was smart, blood smart. He got things done, whatever it took. Pryor Mills didn't walk across a room without purpose. And here he was, if indeed it was him, far from home and his seat of power, in the middle of what was for him nowhere. *My* nowhere.

I was heading out the front door to brace him when Andrea waved at me to hold on, spoke briefly into the phone, then hung up. Linda from Sunny Slope had called to let us know that Mildred Whit was asking for me.

For a couple of years I'd made irregular visits to Sunny Slope. During one of the town's growth spurts, some entrepreneur believed Farr would go on expanding and built an entertainment complex out where the city limits had been projected to extend. City limits stopped short, construction halted, grass and weeds moved in. Finally a local church wrangled the site's donation, boosted further contributions from the community, and established a retirement home.

The Slope had called me in a while back to advise on security issues after their pharmacy was robbed. Better locks, better protocols, and a security camera dealt with that, and in the meanwhile, as I poked about the place, Mrs. Whit took to calling me Hilda, after her youngest daughter. I had a strong feeling she knew I wasn't Hilda, if not initially then certainly further along, but we all tacitly carried on with the pretense. Each visit, her room was my first stop. So, after checking streets front and rear for Pryor Mills or his likeness, I headed out there. On my way I zigzagged through downtown, just in case.

Since my last visit, one of the aides had spruced the room up with a flower vase, a knickknack or two, a new pillowcase and chair cushion, all in shades of the green in which Mrs. Whit often dressed.

"Happy birthday, Mitty," I told her. The charge nurse had cued me.

"Another one," she said. "I'm long out of toes and fingers. And patience."

"They do zip by, don't they?"

"Hummingbirds."

Right. They drop down for a moment, hover and are gone.

"Of course they're nasty little creatures. Always chasing each other away." She took a bite of the tea cake I'd brought, a favorite. An aide had plated a slice, put the rest in the refrigerator for later. Crumbs tumbled onto Mrs. Whit's chin. She looked down to watch them fall from there to her nightgown. "I'm glad you're here."

We sat together as she finished the cake, drank half a cup of tea, and at length fell asleep. I told her I liked what she'd done with the room. She said that was Geri, the new girl, a smart one. Kind young lady even if she didn't know how to spell her own name. She talked about a TV show she watched regularly, with all these characters who kept moving romantically together and apart in implausible permutations. From the sound and content of it I suspect it was nothing current, but a show she'd watched long ago.

The next day there was a call from the Slope. Andrea passed the call to me, a nurse passed the phone to Mrs. Whit. Not a lot of breath behind her words. Pauses fell between and within. She wanted to tell me how much my Thursday visits meant to her. The visits weren't always

Thursday by any means, and hardly regular, just whenever I made it by, but in her mind, yes, Thursdays. Small ceremonies help hold our lives in place.

In the background I heard others speaking. I said I'd be out to see her next week.

She died that night about eleven.

17.

The body was found Tuesday by early-morning hunters out west of town. Been down for something more than a day, something less than two, Doc Gilley said. And damned if he could tell what happened, but there were multiple injuries. One hand was ruined. Recent wounds on head and face. And the man's neck was broken. Clean and quick. A freak accident? I asked. A fall? Doc wore huge glasses that hovered over his face from eyebrows to drooping cheeks. Through them as he moved, you watched the world bend about him, distorted. Could be, he said.

A .38, recently fired, was on the man's belt. Over seven hundred dollars in his wallet and moneyclip.

ID on prints came back before the autopsy was completed. A veteran policeman, Pryor Mills of Kern, New Mexico. KC made the call, speaking with the chief there, who reported Mills as on leave taking personal time. No, he had no knowledge that Officer Mills was traveling out of state, or what his purpose in doing so might be. We couldn't state conclusively what had taken place, KC said, not yet. We'd look into it further, of course, but at the present time considered it an accidental death. One final question. Officer Mills had no identification on him when found. Would the chief have any idea why that might be? And again a no—in a solid parade of them.

KC assured the chief we'd keep him apprised, thanked him again, and hung up.

I told KC he did well. However they're staged, notifications are hard, and never get much easier.

He nodded. "This job, every time you think you've got it covered, another train hits you."

He was right. The playbook sucks. You prepare and prepare, then end up making up most of the moves as you go along.

Mrs. Whit's funeral was that afternoon. Brag, KC, myself, and two caregivers from the Slope attended. One of the Slope employees had brought her kids. From the softspoken exchanges among them she was, I think, doing her best to explain what the service was all about. Brought up Catholic, KC was intrigued by the brevity and plainness of it.

I knocked off early after the funeral, told everyone I'd be on call if they needed me but please don't, and went home hoping to make up for lost time and serial no-shows with Sid. He couldn't shake loose for an hour or so, he said on the phone, so I said I'd make dinner. I never quite realize how much I miss this till I'm back in a kitchen. It had been a long while since that happened, day after day filled with make-dos of apples, cheese, crazy quilt leftovers and (when I could summon sufficient energy and ambition) imaginative sandwiches. The moment onions started sizzling in the pan, my spirits grew lighter. A nice, fluffy omelet, I was thinking, finely grated parmesan inside. Or I could sauté some of that chorizo I had in the freezer, throw in spinach. Maybe a pasta with olives. And when had I last had my hands on fresh figs?

Once you start . . .

Sid's arrival, complete with wine, brought me back. He held out the bottle, swathed halfway up its neck in a paper bag.

"From a friend in Oregon who makes and bottles his own. He warns that the label may be the only remarkable thing about it." Trees against a pale blue sky, bank curving gently down the way a hand might form in air a familiar shape, waters dark and still, patches of reflected sky caught within them.

Actually, the wine itself wasn't bad. Fruity and sweet on the front of the tongue, then fuller. Should age well.

Not this bottle, though. This one went to its final rest as I finished cooking, with Sid sitting at the counter telling me about a case he was working on. Unable to decide, I'd wound up with two entrees going on the stove, so we decided one of them was an appetizer. "Truth, as ever, resides in what we choose to call things," he said.

Which was the tipping point of his case as well.

Real Perry Mason stuff, he said, you bet, this lawyer gig. Witness in the box, judge peering down from on high, music low in the background as cameras hold their breath . . . when what's really going on is, you're sitting on your butt twelve to fourteen hours a day stalking statutes, precedents, prior rulings, relevances. For everything good you grab hold of, there's something as not-good or worse a step or two further along. Oh the drama of it! The humanity!

"Hmmmm. Perry Mason."

"A classic."

"For old farts fallen prey to nostalgia."

"Or a bright memory in the murky lives of lawyers who start out to save the world and end up assailed by doubt."

"Not only lawyers, Sid."

"Of course."

Food was done, and I downloaded it to serving platters.

"Which one's the appetizer?" Sid asked.

"The one on the left."

"Your left or mine?"

"Eye of the beholder."

"Well, in that case . . ." He spooned equal servings of each onto both our plates. We ate as he went on telling me about Charlotte Hoy, court-committed following the murder of her lover, Adele Fourier, nine years ago.

"Her contention, her lawyer's at any rate, is not only that she remains innocent of the murder as she has insisted all along, but also that, following treatment and release, by definitions implicit in the statements of her attending physicians she's a different person, and asks that the court recognize such by severing any and all connections to her prior identity."

"This is something more than word play? And commas?"

"I know, seems simple. Shazam, you're a new person. But it begs fundamental issues."

"I don't get it."

"She won't, either. This probably won't ever be heard. But she, the lawyer—someone—is pushing hard."

"It's not like she's asking for absolution. What would she hope to gain?"

"We don't know. But seemingly small decisions can have vast, unforeseen repercussions."

"And you're on the side of?"

"It's hard even to get a fix on what the sides are. Nobody's been there before."

"Dragons and tygers. But I heard a *we* tucked away in there."

"I'm doing research for the judge who may be hearing this. Read, read. Scribble, scribble. Scroll, scroll . . . More appetizer?"

"Pass. A bit more of the entrée, though."

"This poor spoon and I hover in indecision."

So I pointed.

"I knew you'd come around."

Sid got up to make coffee for us.

"The whole affair seems a bit fantastical."

He turned back from the sink, carafe half filled. "It does. One longs for the moment the drama drains away, Perry's explained everything, and all is well with the world again." He set up the coffee maker as I finished eating and carted dishes to the sink.

"You haven't heard the most fantastical part."

"Okay."

"The name she wishes to be known by is Adele Fourier. Her murdered lover's."

That night I couldn't sleep, finally got up and went in to look over the file on Pryor Mills. KC was on the swing to graveyard. About eleven he came knocking at my door, with a package.

"FedEx dropped this off right after you left."

I thanked him and, when he lingered, asked if there was something else.

"Guess there is, Sarah. This—"he pointed to the folders on my desk—"is heavy stuff. People wonder why you're not taking lead on it."

"People, as in you?"

"I'd be in the line, yeah."

"Any reason you *shouldn't* be lead?"

"No, ma'am."

"You're ready for it?"

"I hope so."

"Everything I see here's solid, KC, one foot in front of the other while keeping watch off to the sides. A steady go."

"I don't know . . ."

"You think I was ready to run this show the day I fell into it?"

"Yes ma'am, I do."

"If only I shared that confidence, then or now. Which puts you and me in much the same place."

He smiled and pulled out his phone to check the time, ignoring the clock on the wall behind him. "Thanks for that, Sarah. Time for me to do the midnight drive-round. Show citizens their police force is on the job."

"Brag just had the car serviced. Enjoy it while you can."

"Truth is, I may miss the rattles and hiccups. Two in the morning, they do help keep you awake."

"Maybe next time we can ask Sonny to leave a few of them in."

"Oh, they'll be back soon enough."

The package had only a POB number as return address. Inside the padded envelope was one of those bound composition books with ruled pages and mottled black-and-white covers. I recognized the handwriting immediately.

The world goes on out there. Interestingly enough, it does fine without you. This seems inevitable and at the same time not right at all. Every thought we carry around with us floats above its capsized reflection.

Several pages further along:

A voyage around my room, with its two chairs, table, bookshelves, narrow bed, would take four minutes, or forever. I rarely leave the room, go for weeks without hearing another voice, looking upon another face. Yet some of the most interesting times (who could possibly have guessed?) are those when I look around, perhaps at the gouged-out grout of the kitchen tile or the sagging window casement, or listen to the floorboards groan as I walk over them, and for a moment, for just one fantastic, exhilarating moment, I don't know where I am.

The dust of my history, of memory, lies on every surface.

———

Back the only time in my life I ever watched TV, back in rehab, there were these same three or four supposedly grand ideas that got plugged in, like pivots, in damn near every script, every show.

Do the right thing, yet another intense fool would say. So simple. As if a person would know. As if, right or wrong, or somewhere in between (that narrow strip of land we live on), there would not be disastrous consequences.

And, in cop shows, all those scenes in interrogation rooms? Whenever the interrogateds say I don't know what you're talking about? They always do.

———

Even as a child it seemed to me undeniable. Whatever it is – land, camels, slaves, gold, even knowledge – there's only so much of it. If A has more, B has accountably less. The currency changes, but whoever has more of it has power. It really is that simple. What is not simple is how, in one's daily life, one navigates this.

Many of the notebook's 23 filled pages comprised such, each line entered without correction or emendation as though shaped in thought well before pen, or in this case pencil, met paper. Most of the rest dealt with Cal's chaotic, sense-jangled return from the war, including actions that horrified him now.

The final entry read:

I realized this morning that it no longer seems important to go on with this. Whatever I believed this would accomplish has either taken place or failed. I suppose it will be some time before I know, if ever I do.

Sitting in Cal's chair I looked up at Cal's wall, Cal's poster, remembering our visit to the house when he disappeared, how he lived in that single room, how featureless the entire house was. How, in a later visit, I sat watching sunlight pool on bed and floor, hearing the sound of wasps in their nest two rooms away. We never can know another person, can we?

I've been on the job maybe five months and Cal and I are in his car riding out to the Beecher farm in response to a missing child call. I'm driving. Mostly we're batting the same old balls over the same old nets the way you do, stuff going on around town, the new grocery store coming in, Doc Edgar retiring, when the conversation takes a turn.

"You've done well, Sarah."

"Thank you."

"Thing is, you're meant for this."

"Pretty sure I'm not."

"Don't ever be sure about anything." He pauses, looks out the side window at a pond with dozens of dragonflies flitting above it. "I've been meaning to tell you this. Now that I've watched you work, the way you move in and out of situations, how you approach people, those aren't things that get taught, they're in you or they're not."

"I try."

"See, that's what I mean. You don't try, you do. Instinctively."

"Most days I'm in way over my head, Cal."

"Of course you are. We're all in over our heads, from day one." He points ahead. "Turn's there where the fence breaks off for a couple yards."

I take a left onto a dirt road that's hard and smooth as asphalt. Took some work. House and barn, when we get there, are every bit as well maintained.

"I look at all that, and with what you've told me," Cal says, "I can't help but wonder if I checked your background, what I'd come up with."

"I never understood why you didn't."

"I know everything I need to."

18.

Sid had been out of town on a consulting job, unhappy with the travel involved but glad to get a break from the Charlotte Hoy case, and returned bearing a sweatshirt that read I WAS NEVER THERE. But he'd brought me a real present as well, he said, a copy of *Times Square Red, Times Square Blue,* one of the books that helped him understand what cities are, how they continually buck and heave beneath us and how, day by day, we adapt to live in them. So as Sid and I ate an improvised pasta and drained a bottle of Sonoma county Meritage, we talked about how cities and towns, these small nations, become entities. Tired entities that *we* were, that was pretty much the extent of our reunion and of intellectual discourse.

Alarms, domestic disputes, bar fights, traffic mishaps, squatters in an abandoned housing development outside town, city council meetings that seemed to issue from some alternate universe. Normal times, such as they are. I'd got used to being in over my head. I'd learned to breathe down there. I had gills.

A follow-up call from the police chief in New Mexico proved, if not forthcoming, then suggestive. He listened as KC passed along official autopsy results (multiple wounds on face and limbs, all occurring pre mortem, evidence of binding, broken neck) before confiding that Officer Mills's personal time had in fact been administrative leave. The chief deftly sidestepped further disclosure. A single moment of candor, the rest fancy footwork.

Privately, Doc Gilley told KC the broken neck came quick and sure, but before that, possibly for some time, a . . . dialog had taken place.

KC followed me into my office that morning with coffee for both of us. He'd overstayed his shift to see me. This was interesting. We peered at one another over the rims of our cups. Spaghetti Western music would not have been out of place. Long, slow hold on the close-ups.

"I called back to New Mexico late last night, Sarah. Waited till I knew the chief would be gone, thought maybe I'd be able to talk, grunt to grunt. Hope that's okay."

"Why wouldn't it be? You're the investigating officer."

"That's what I used as my opening. New at this, boots way too big, feet sliding around in them. With the boss watching every step I take."

Good move. I was proud of my boy. They grow up so fast.

He'd spoken with an Officer Guzman. Late twenties from the sound of his voice, remnants of Spanish there too. Mills? Sure. Been in the department a long time, trained more than half of them. Not around so much anymore, since that detective thing.

KC slid forward in his chair.

"I knew that was my thread, Sarah. The 'detective thing.' I pulled at it, hard."

Within the month KC and I had switched places, him behind the desk and me before. He sat back there still tugging that thread, still feeling the need to go on apologizing, while the interchange continued much as before.

"Pryor Mills and Brian Hubble came up together as friends, served stateside in the army on separate coasts, Mills as an MP, then returned to Kern, joined the police force there. Just over eight years ago detective Hubble sustained an attack by an unknown assailant."

KC was watching for tics, of course. Reaction, eye movement, small changes.

"Mills found him, unresponsive, barely breathing at all. He'd vomited and aspirated—plus, his neck and trachea had been severely damaged in the attack. He was on a ventilator a while, got off but remained in full-blown coma for months, then unexpectedly revived and foundered along for ten or eleven months before sinking back. About two years ago, he drifted up again before going under to stay, with only one last, brief rally. His wife had also disappeared the night of the incident, possibly taken by the attacker, possibly . . . Who knows, my informant said. But Pryor Mills stayed with the man, talked to him, helped take care of him, right to the end."

KC sat quietly. Leave space, I'd told him. People will speak into silence.

He looked toward the window.

"There's no record of a Sarah Jane Pullman in New Mexico, or back where you say you're from."

"No."

"The name change must have been immediately after."

"It was."

At the time, his thoughts more aligned to guilt, betrayal, and self-doubt, KC could have had no intimation how much I admired the skills he'd shown. I was able to tell him later, once we'd swapped places again, before he died.

"You really didn't know, did you, Sarah? What happened."

"My intention was only to put him down and get away—alive. Having done that, I kept as much distance between as I could."

"You never checked back?"

"Leave bread crumbs, and sooner or later someone's going to follow them."

He ducked his head, then met my eyes. "That's a lot to carry around, Sarah."

"We all have weight."

"I don't believe—"

That I killed Mills? "Of course you do. You have to."

"And I have to remember how all this time you've told me we can't ever know another person, that anyone's capable of anything given the right push."

He'd started to say something more when the phone rang. He answered without a greeting, responded with a yes, an okay and a no before hanging up.

"Sorry." He scribbled a note, two, maybe three words. "Others want me to bring in the state police."

"That would be appropriate."

"It's my call. Not that it should be. Not that I want it to be, or have any business sitting here."

"I always felt the same way. We should be cautious of any who don't."

"Little of what I just said is written down, Sarah, not in any kind of straight line."

I waited. "So is that all for now?"

"You'll be at home? If I need you?"

"Of course."

The more time I spent at home free of cluttered days, the larger the space, my world, grew, not smaller as one might expect. That space began to edge toward boundless, in fact. The question as ever being, Did I grow with it, or shrink in proportion?

Or was I merely going daft and wonky from too much time alone?

After all these years away from it, with Sid I had slowly returned to cooking. And now, with free time my daylong companion, I jumped in full-hearted, no mercy asked or given. Tracks of flour on face, T-shirt and shorts, butter smears everywhere, sink piled with mixing bowls, utensils, measuring cups and spoons, containers of baking powder, spices, yeast and sugar sitting open and vulnerable. All this with no one, save Sid upon occasion, to cook for. Gained weight wasn't yet showing on the scales, but I could hear it hissing loudly in my ear.

"You could feed whole troops with this," Sid said after a single glance at the kitchen one night when he came by for dinner.

So that's what I did. Monday, Wednesday and Friday I cooked dinner for the residents at Sunny Slope, Mildred Whit's old haunt, ate with them, and hung around after to help clean up. Before long, others joined and we had a stable of volunteers.

"You're to blame," I told Sid, who'd become one of those volunteers.

"A blame I'll happily accept." He spooned another, smaller helping of cheese grits onto his plate. "Deserved or not."

Other than that reboot (*Remember me, dear court-bouillon?*) my days were like bobbing logs that people in wonderfully bad movies have to use to cross stretches of water. Regardless the degree of skill or caution, the way across is iffy, keeping balance is everything. KC showed up regularly, not to ask questions about the homicide but to keep me apprised, and to solicit advice concerning other matters: the town's ordinance on display advertising, what the hell the mayor might be thinking, a newly formed home-owner's association, the first of its kind locally.

A second, long-abandoned pleasure got salvaged as well, starting with the book Sid brought me, moving along to visits with familiars from college days then to others, indiscriminately, everything from Alexandre Dumas to Zora Neale Hurston and Joanna Russ. Not long after, I became intrigued by vintage cooking gear and began haunting junk shops, Goodwill, and yard sales for copper pans, coffee per-colators, depression glass, tinware. At that point, figuring I wasn't far this side of ruin, I grew concerned. Next I'd be taking up knitting, or golf, or butterfly collecting. Wake up one morning with shelves full of porcelain figurines of shepherds.

A story I read back then was about a Neanderthal who lived into the present. He had a shack down an alley, sur-vived doing simple odd jobs, kept low and in the shadows, hugging the earth. His was a dim world. Everyone around him was smarter, quicker, lighter, faster. They all belonged. Most mornings I looked around and knew exactly how he felt.

19.

I have dates, times and details of the investigation logged, but in writing this I've declined to refer to them. Points on a line can never approach the experience itself. And even as you pick it up to have a closer look, the past changes.

KC came by Sunny Slope one evening just as daylight was letting go, to tell me they'd found Cal's body. We were serving dinner, shepherd's pie fortified with spinach, a salad of iceberg lettuce, cucumber, and poached pears. Toeing the line between comfort food and what residents would consider if not highfalutin then certainly falutin of some sort.

It was a motel out on the old two-lane highway, nine cabins, his the last, "not much but snakes and weeds past it." Paradise Inn, with a couple letters, the first *a* and the *d*, gone MIA from the sign long ago. Two weeks back he'd paid in cash for the month. Three, maybe four days ago he'd filled the tub, hung a tarp on the corner wall, carefully positioned the shotgun, and per his poster joined the 44 veterans who committed suicide in the time we spend talking about some celebrity's tummy tuck. The owner was in the back of the office with a TV going loud and never heard anything. He found Cal not too long after the flies did.

Still shaken, KC had as much trouble telling me this as I had hearing it.

"Is there somewhere we can go, Sarah?"

I turned everything over to the volunteers. KC and I stepped outside, to a patio that saw more use from pigeons than from residents. Always my favorite time of day, half-light, half-dark, could as easily be morning as evening. As though the day were holding its breath, undecided, all potential.

"We thought Cal was long gone."

KC nodded. "I think he was, for a while. You hadn't heard more from him, right?"

"Only that one call. How was I doing, how's the town getting along. A wave goodbye, really."

I brought up the other calls with no one on the line, what Laura Chen had said about an old friend looking for me, my neighbor's seeing someone at the house. The shuffling of papers on my refrigerator door.

"Which could have been Cal," KC said. "All that."

"Or Mills."

"Or no one. Nothing."

In part because it was what I had from Cal that was mine alone, from a kind of miserliness, I didn't bring up the notebook. *Whenever the interrogateds say I don't know what you're talking about? They always do.*

KC held out a sheet of paper. "This is a copy, Sarah."

Done on our ancient photocopy machine, whose copies came out blurry, as though you were reading them through clouded water. You could see the ragged edge to the left, where the copied page had been torn from the notebook sent me or one like it.

"This was on the bed in Cal's room, held in place by a shoe."

There's no way I'm about to write down any of the usual crap here: asking your forgiveness, hope you can understand, diddle-diddle, cow jumped over the moon. I don't really give a shit whether you understand, or what. As for forgiveness, keep it for yourself. You're going to need it. We all do.

Something kept bringing me back. I don't know how many times I left, then some morning or night I'd get up, step outside, and here I was.

Which brings me to what I do give a shit about.

This town.

Pryor Mills needed killing, as much as any man I ever knew. Came into this town, no respect for it or for any of us, leaving his muddy footprints and his spit and his smell everywhere, one of our own in his sights. His last dumb idea in what I figure was a lifetime of them.

I think I'm done now.

I handed back the copy. "Does this sound like Cal to you, even remotely?"

"What I'm thinking is, he had reason to be watching over you. Saw something, knew something we don't. I thought Mills was here to carry out his friend's final request. He could have had his own agenda."

Settled on the lowest branch of a nearby elm, a squirrel with its chitter, patient till then, began questioning our right to be there.

"I've got as much respect for Cal as anyone does. He had a history, though, we all know that. And that's not even figuring in the way he left, here one day, gone the next." KC held up the note. "I read this, what it sounds like to me is some parts have come loose inside him, they're in there spinning free, not catching. And he knew it."

"It's not a confession, KC."

"Of course it is."

The squirrel had come to ground and moved in closer, tail waving rhythmically in concert with its *kuk, kuk, kuk*.

"It's time for you to get back to work, Sarah."

"I appreciate everything you've done, KC. But that's not a good idea."

Time passed, which may be the one thing you can rely on. I managed to fill days, if baggily: books, long walks, cooking, AA-level coffee-drinking, apples, a glass of wine, more cooking. It took a week before I stopped answering phone or doorbell. People would stand there, or sit there, mouthing the same things. On impulse one Friday, I threw some things in the backseat and drove the sixty-odd miles up to Dunlap to spend a weekend with Sid. Even the road, so often traversed, looked different. Everything had changed.

Including, as it happened, the fluid borders between Sid and myself. That night we went out to his favorite bar for a drink, to dinner near the capitol at a restaurant whose menu in its heft resembled a Dickens novel, then to a coffee shop in what until recently had been a Korean neighborhood and was fast becoming a center for galleries, artist studios, live music, theater. By midday Saturday we both felt wordless spaces forming between us. Neither of us spoke of them; to do so would be to make those spaces material, give them substance.

"You don't have to be here," Sid finally said, far into the night. A party was going on three houses down. The music's bass thumped like our own heartbeats. We watched the lash of headlights as cars came and went.

Sid stood and turned to me, hand raised, finger angled skyward, and for that moment, as headlights swept over him, for that single, transient moment, he was beautiful, isolate, part of another, better world.

Forty minutes outside Farr, my headlights fell on what I thought to be a person walking beside the road, but when I pulled over, yards further along before I could slow and stop, no one was there. Nothing. I shut the car off and got out. Only a faint breath of wind in the trees and, low against the horizon, first light, or promise of same. The kind of morning Daddy and I might have headed into the woods to hunt, shotguns broke open and hung across crooked elbows.

KC was backing out of my driveway as I turned the corner at Sycamore. He stopped the van, got out, and came over. Didn't give me time to get the door open. I rolled the window down.

"Been looking everywhere for you." No smile, no greeting. Minutes past six in the morning. "I need your help."

"And I need coffee."

He followed me inside, talking the while, much of it at first failing to pierce the fog of my lack of sleep and shadowed thoughts.

Daniel Hopf, fourteen, had gone missing, twenty hours

and counting. He'd attended a church function—at the vacant field by the Lutheran church? Saturdays, they host pick-up ball games and other such events—and as usual was to walk home after, but he never showed up there. The mother, divorced, father living in Austin, Texas, had called the church, talked to parents of the boy's friends, driven by the field and by the old newsstand where he sometimes stopped to browse through magazines. Then she'd called us.

I let that *us* go without comment.

So far, KC said, he'd followed in the mother's tracks. Church, friends, regular route. Then the hospital. Registered offenders. Came up empty.

Changing his mind, KC poured a cup of coffee. He tilted his head toward the wall by the sink. "You have mice."

Scratching. Which I'd got so used to, I didn't hear it anymore.

"Never lonely," I said. "Never without friends."

"That's true, even if you don't believe it. Great coffee."

"What can I say? I'm a cook. We know things. Secret things. Put sauce on Spam, smash it all together, call it paté."

KC looked tired. Or maybe I was tired and seeing it in him.

"Ever feel like everything's broken, Sarah?"

"Oh yeah."

KC rinsed his cup and put it on the rack by the sink. "So what else can we do?"

First *us*, now *we*. I'd been conscripted. And truth to tell,

I was bone tired of second pots of coffee, third goes at Jane Austen or Brontë novels, and bowls of cassoulet that could have fed a family of four.

Back during college days I read a story about an artist who, following yet another failed affair, opens the veins of her wrist with an Exacto knife and in the afterlife finds herself in a vast commons room like those of state hospitals and prisons, thousands of souls tucked into chairs along the wall watching old shows on TV, doing crossword puzzles, reminiscing, napping, zoned out—thousands upon thousands with their own fogs, their own confusion, their own feeling that somehow they've been profoundly cheated or betrayed. Given the choice of staying there as she is or returning to life as an insect, she imagines herself as some kind of beetle, a cockroach maybe. At the end of the story, either in actuality or in her imagination, she's lying on her back, feet paddling at the air for a purchase that will forever elude her.

20.

A lot is made in novels, American novels in particular, it seems, of the notion of redemption. Something someone's done lurches up out of the past, or that someone does it as we watch, and the next 160 or 800 pages show the scrambling back to balance. That's what my college teachers kept pointing out, anyhow. Maybe it was a sign of the times, the nation's common soul flashing guilts it needed to pick up and put down elsewhere, teachers finding redemption in books because that's what they were looking for. Or maybe I'm overthinking this whole thing.

At any rate, clearly I was still thinking not only about what I'd been reading but also about my own patchwork past.

All that as I followed up leads on fourteen-year-old Daniel Hopf, which felt like double vision. I told KC I'd help, with the understanding that such help was temporary. And while I was weary of hours stretching out like southwest mesas, flat, bare, endless, I also demurred at giving up my . . . my what? Freedom's definitely not the word. Safe harbor, maybe. Refuge.

Daniel seemed to be one of those kids whose friends were all circumstantial. Some from his church, others from community events sponsored by the Lutheran church though it wasn't his, those with whom he shared classrooms at school or knew from his neighborhood. None of them particularly close as far as I could tell, none he hung out with.

One name did come up, that of a boy two years older, Malcolm, who sounded to be as fundamentally disconnected as Daniel himself. I was shown to his room apologetically—to myself and Malcolm in equal parts—by his mother. White butcher's paper covered the lower half of windows, itself half-covered with words and figures from a flat carpenter's pencil nearby. Decorative ledges along the top of each wall had been subverted to bookshelves. A vintage electronic organ sat propped off plumb on a side table with one short leg.

"Sure, I know him. Skinny kid, thick middle, walks like he's wearing snow boots. He's a weird one. Why?"

I had to wonder what might score as weird in Malcolm's world. He was feeding something in a cage, a ferret from the smell, standing in front such that I couldn't make out what it was.

"He's missing."

"Missing what?"

"As in, he never got home on Saturday and no one knows where he is."

"Not good."

"That's our feeling as well. Not to mention his mother's."

"Sorry for her. But it's not like the boy and I are buds, ma'am, just neither of us stays up on the latest thing, you know? So, two outriders, we have to be tight, right?"

"Then you don't have any idea where he might go? A favorite place, some activity others wouldn't know about . . ."

"I know he has a friend, someone older. Talked about her once when we ran into each other at the library. We'd both got interested in fungus, me for about ten minutes, him a lot longer, and were by the same shelves reading up on it."

"A friend. That's what he said?"

Malcolm stepped away from the cage. *Two* ferrets. Busily scarfing up food while watching him closely, ever alert to the possibility of better or, barring that, more. "Not like what you're thinking. Someone who helped settle things down when they got runny, is what he said. No name, no. But she must have lived near him, from the way he talked."

I thanked Malcolm and his mother and was off to criss-cross Daniel Hopf's neighborhood. Generally when neighborhoods go down they do so on an ever-steeper decline, and stay. This was a rare one, visibly on its way back up. Considerable care had been turned toward restoring and maintaining the original mid-level housing.

Well-worn and webbed with cracks, streets and curbs were clean of debris. Ambitious real estate agents might find the area lacking in their beloved curb appeal, but it all looked good to me as I went house to house.

The fourteenth door I knocked at, 1534 Pell Street, four blocks from his home, was opened by Daniel Hopf himself. I asked for the owner.

"I'm sorry, Rebecca's unavailable. Could I help you?" He had on a windbreaker and watch cap. Inside, I understood why. It was maybe 65 degrees in there. Curtains drawn closed all around. Light came from a single table lamp with something on the order of a 40-watt bulb.

I told him who I was, why I was there, and was told in turn that his friend had been having a bad time of it, an especially bad time, that there was no way he could leave her alone like this, and that he'd just phoned his parents, which he'd not done before because they would have made him leave if they'd known, to say he was sorry and would be home soon, now that Becky was over the worst of it. Sorry about the cold, he said. It helps, she feels better this way. Heat gets to her. And light hurts her eyes. He hoped everyone would forgive him all the bother and worry he'd put them through.

Rebecca Post had cancer. "Just your ordinary, garden variety, boring, shared-with-eight-million-other-people cancer." After multiple runs of chemo and radiation and two operations, she made the decision to call it quits, signed up for hospice care, and had been living at home for five months. Meals on Wheels brought food daily, not that she was able to eat much of anything. Specialist nurses visited weekly. She had okay days and really, really bad days. These last were some of the worst. And Danny was a blessing.

"I asked him to go home. *Told* him to, more than once. But he has a mind of his own, that boy."

A humidifier in one corner pumped away so heartily that you felt the dampness as you entered, like stepping into a cold rainforest, and caught your breath. A sour, bitter smell hung in the room, maybe from the machine, maybe from Rebecca herself. Urine in the bag at bedside was a dark yellow-brown, so the smell could be from meds as well. Worn or off level, the humidifier's fan ticked with each round.

They'd met at the library, she told me, while she was reading up on everything she could find about cancer and he was looking for information about yurts because he wondered what *home* meant in different cultures. Had a curiosity to match his stubbornness.

I explained that the library was where Daniel had met Malcolm, the young man who sent me her way, as well, and that Daniel at that time had been researching fungus.

She asked if I'd ever seen the movie *Harold and Maude* and when I said I hadn't, told me it was a little like that, the most unlikely of friendships between a far older woman and a young boy, set apart by their character types as much as by age. He started coming over almost every day after school on his way home, sometimes dropped by in the morning just to be sure she was okay.

By then KC was there, thanking me far too effusively and telling Daniel how worried his mother was.

After KC and Daniel left for his home and I'd told Rebecca to call if she needed anything, I got in the rattly old Chevy pickup I'd bought when my city car left me and was halfway to the office before I realized it. One of those form and content things. Do the work, go through the motions, switches get thrown. Act like a sheriff, you start thinking you are one.

I shook my head at old habits, turned around, and went home. Back to the yurt.

Eight in the morning, no one should be knocking at the door. Of course, as far as I was concerned, no time was good for knocking at my door. I'd disconnected the doorbell weeks ago and decided that any such knocks belonged to a woodpecker doing its thing somewhere. Of no concern to me.

But this woodpecker wouldn't stop. So I pulled on enough of yesterday's clothes to get by, opened the door, and stood there letting my displeased expression serve as greeting.

Young man in bad suit. Probably not that young, but everyone was beginning to look that way to me. Nor was the suit out of line with what people wore on Sundays hereabouts. In bright sunlight it was either dark blue or gray. I was trying to make out which as, oblivious to my displeasure, he went on talking, having begun, I'd swear, before I could get the door fully open.

Sentence by drawling sentence I came to realize that not only had someone broached my door at eight in the morning, and not only had I foolishly answered the door, but I had opened the door to, of all things, a lawyer. One who wished to represent me in a lawsuit against the city, well-polished phrases such as wrongful termination and lack of due process stumbling over one another in their haste to leave his tongue. One who would not be redirected, even slowed, by my declaration that I had no complaint against the city nor, insofar as I knew, the city against me.

Did he actually say Power is never given up, it's always taken, or am I cutting to fit? Memory loves a good story.

Dead certain that's when I started laughing, though. Power in this context being laughable. Or worse. A groaner.

"Oh. Well, then . . ." Upon which he stopped talking and looked around, as though wondering where he might be and how he came to be there. A man who, venturing out near the break of dawn on a fool's mission, must have as precious little to attend to as myself.

I suggested that coffee would be a boon to both of us.

"Well, sure . . ."

And who was every bit as decisive.

He stood surveying shelves, no doubt wondering why anyone would have six kinds of coffee makers, while I, busy with beans and grinder, watched in the window over the sink wondering yet again how men can look in mirrors day after day and never notice eyebrows beginning to resemble jungle undergrowth and hair sprouting out of their ears.

"So, what? Keeping the world a just and honorable place is going slow right now?"

He laughed. Not a very committed laugh, but it found its way out. Good. I'd been worried for him.

He looked back at the shelves. Colanders of every size, a mandoline, pasta maker, choppers, a stack of rolled silicon mats. "I don't know what half that stuff up there is. But you're sure as hell neat."

"Tools—I used to be a cook. My father was the sort who could build a house, wire it, do the plumbing, brick up a sidewalk or entryway, drop in doors and windows. Had every tool he needed, every one of them with its place. 'The socket wrench lives here,' he'd say when I wasn't much taller than one of his handsaws. 'And the crescent ought to be right next to it, but it slipped over there and settled down one day when I wasn't paying attention.'"

"So you got that from him."

"Like so much else. What about your family?"

The coffee was ready. I put a cup before him, which he tried before responding. Nodded in appreciation.

"Standard issue small-town. High school sweethearts,

married after graduation, bought a house half a mile from where they were born. Went to work, stayed in place there too. Not much evidence they ever considered anything else."

"They got you off to college, though. Law school."

"Something did. Restlessness, maybe."

"Yet you came back here."

"I did. *Why*'s a big question."

"Always."

He ran his finger along the table's edge. "Don't know when I last saw one of these."

"We had one just like it when I was a kid." Oval shaped, moss-green formica top, corrugated aluminum band around the side, chrome legs. "It was second- or third-hand even then. Couldn't tell if the top was stained from use or supposed to look like that. Took this place the minute I saw the table."

"Some the worse for wear."

"And still earning its keep."

"Right. Could I?" Holding up his cup.

I got the carafe, poured for us both. We sat quietly, one of those rare, flickering moments of peace closing about us.

"My girlfriend and I, Nanor, we've been together nine years. She works for the newspaper, writes up whatever needs doing. Most of it's anonymous. Club luncheons, school sports events, city council meetings, court reports. She says you've done a lot for the town—"

"Not really."

"—and for women."

"Even less."

"She'd disagree."

"She doesn't know much about me."

"Only what she's seen day to day."

"What people see has as much to do with themselves as with what they're looking at. But I can tell you how it feels. For every gain you make, there's slippage somewhere else. Sometimes the slippage is bigger than the gain."

"True enough." He finished his coffee and stood. "Best I go look to foment some slippage myself. Thanks for seeing me. It got to be important to me—for reasons I don't particularly understand."

"You're not trolling for a client, then."

"There's no way you'd consider bringing action against the town."

"Despite that grand opening spiel."

"I went over it four or five times on the way here. Hoping it would keep you from slamming the door in my face. If you opened it at all."

I held out my hand. "Your name?"

"Oh. Sorry. I was so intent on . . ." He laughed, closer to the real thing this time. "Horace Tanner."

"Not exactly a standard-issue small-town name, Horace."

"Epic, huh? And I don't have a clue where it came from."

21.

Dr. Balducci once spoke of one of *his* teachers, quoting an editor that teacher admired, who'd said of words when they played well together: "There is a small revolution going on in that sentence."

In class it brought on a period-long discussion of what language could do, its undertows and subterfuge, and now had me thinking over documents from my life: diary, court records, service discharge, letters and emails, job applications, legal papers, Cal's notebook. From anybody's life. How some documents bolster what we know and believe, some fly in the face of it.

I mean, you'd think the whole life would be in there. But take all those documents of a person's life and put them in a line, connect the dots, what are you likely to wind up with? How many images, and how different? Like artists' sketches in TV crime shows. One witness squints at it and says Hell, that could be anybody, the next says it doesn't look like anyone at all.

In short, each sentence, each document, *is* a small revolution, tearing into the one before, reshaping it.

"There's no way you needed my help," I told KC when he came calling later that day. As usual I'd filled time with— now that I think of it, I can't say what I'd filled time with. Nothing much that I can recall. But hours fell away and KC was at the door as light softened and cicadas started up. Most cicadas sing during the day. These were Northern Dusk-Singers, they love twilight, and we had droves of them. "You and Brag were good to go. Hell, Daniel wasn't even missing, he'd just stepped out of the room. *Ploy* comes to mind."

"What smells so good?"

"There's a pear tart in the oven. Come on out, I've got coffee brewing to go with."

He followed me to the kitchen. Beneath the smell of the tart lay that of olives and garlic from last night's hurriedly improvised pasta, a dwelling dampness, cleansers.

We drank coffee as the tart cooled.

"Had a visit from your FBI boy today," KC said.

"Tyrell Martin."

"That's the one. He was curious what I'd been up to in New Mexico. Seemed to think it was some business of his."

"Beautiful country over that way."

"It is for sure."

I got up and cut two slices, poured more coffee.

"Thought you might want to know too," KC said.

"No more my business than his, is it?"

"Hard to say."

KC held his fork overhand. He didn't quite manage to keep his mouth closed while chewing.

"Damn that's good."

"The chef I got it from said what you do is take pie and remove everything that's not essential."

Five forkfuls and he was done. I didn't ask, just cut him another slice.

"I left things with Brag for a couple of days and drove over. You know how it gets to be, Sarah, too many tent ropes flapping loose in the wind. Figured I'd check in, find out more about this Mills fellow."

KC dug into his second slice before going on.

"Where I wound up was at the hospital, the one this detective Brian Hubble died at, with a nurse who took care of him. Roy Hammond, a medic who came home after discharge and went to nursing school, been at the hospital ever since. One leg's a couple inches short from breaks that went too long before getting treated. Shoulders, arms, chest look like they belong to someone half again his size and half his age. Lot of that's from rehab after the leg got fixed, he says. Then years of lifting patients, helping them in and out of chairs, beds, off the floor.

"Hammond was one of Hubble's primary caretakers the

last two years, says he probably got to know Pryor Mills as well as anyone could, Mills being the kind, when you reached out, nothing came back. No question he was devoted to his friend, though. Stood by him all those years Hubble was in a coma, and he was there that last time when his friend came out of it, when it was like a different man had got up into that bed. He remembers being in the room right at the end when Hubble asked Mills to do something for him. Go find her for me, he said. Please. Your wife, you mean, Mills said. Hubble nodded. Find her and tell her I'm sorry. Tell her I forgive her.

"Hammond says it looked to him like Mills didn't much care for that. But he agreed. Said 'I'll find her all right.'"

Between us we'd killed the pot of coffee, which worked out close to four cups apiece. The cicadas had quieted, and my mockingbird took over. He was reeling out phrase after phrase, some raggedly melodic, others raucous, all fragmentary. With the caffeine in my system, I felt pretty damn raucous myself.

"That wasn't anything I expected to hear," KC said.

"And?"

"Fuck if I know." He looked down, then back up. "Sorry. But the more information you have, the plainer things are supposed to get, not more complicated."

"Does this change what you think?"

"It has to, doesn't it?"

"You still think Cal killed Pryor Mills? That his note supports that?"

Silence filled the room, only for seconds, but we both felt its presence, before KC said, "As much as I ever did."

See you at work tomorrow were KC's jestful parting words, and I woke the next morning to find myself, though I'd consciously made no such decision, with my mind tilting that way.

By nine I was behind the desk with a cup of coffee and several months's worth of paperwork KC had been thoughtful enough to preserve for me in a stack as precisely aligned as cards in a deck.

Why did I come back to this?

Mayor Baumann dropped by to say it was good I was here, a councilman and councilwoman (the latter, rumor had it, considering a run for mayor in the next election), old Doc Newmann, then a promoter who appeared to have in mind some kind of festival or fair out at the Meadors place, which was all I got from his pitch since, four or five steps in, each sentence strayed far off the path. I asked him to submit a formal proposal in writing. That usually does it.

KC and I had gone down the street for breakfast when I showed up, easing small talk back and forth across the table like pieces in a board game as we ate. The weight of the conversation changed only once, as we ambled back to the office. "You ever want to talk to me about it, Sarah . . ." He left the rest unsaid.

Two MPs, straight as fenceposts, polite as oldtime railroad porters, came calling that afternoon. Billy Crestwood had gone AWOL. They were here to fetch him. Their lieutenant had advised a courtesy call to local law and, Billy's being backwoods folk, I suggested it might be well for me to accompany them. We drove out to the family house. Even from a distance you could see the house's second floor had been long uninhabitable; below, plywood and cement blocks abounded. The land, once prize farmland, was mostly dirt and scrub.

Billy's grandfather met us well away from the house to say no sir, he hadn't seen Billy, and no one else had neither, and yes, he did mind if the two armies had a look around but they might as well go ahead, seeing as they were so flat-out determined.

The MPs searched and found no sign of Billy, overlooking, as it happened, the single imprint of a new, hard sole on the back porch. Billy was there somewhere, no doubt about it, but I said nothing.

As we drove away, one of the MPs asked me how many people lived there. They'd lost count, he said, of those stepping out as they entered rooms and spaces.

Depends was the only answer I had for them.

That was it for the day, as far as actual police work went. I bum-rushed the paperwork, chatted with Brag and with Andrea out front, hoofed it down to the diner halfway through the afternoon for a sandwich, as much to hang with

Gracie and the regulars as for food. Would have dragged KC with me but he was out on a traffic call.

Probably the pivot point, that day. By the end of the week I admitted to myself how little I was seeing of KC. Mornings, he'd check in, come or call in during the shift when he had anything to report or follow up on, appear in my doorway if he had a question, otherwise seemed always to be away or on his way there. When he showed up one night around six, with most everybody out front gone for the day, I wasn't surprised, I'd been expecting it. He took the seat across from the desk that no one ever used. I closed the computer and leaned back. I could hear the soughing of our central air and sounds of light traffic out on Hob Street. They seemed equally distant.

"I'm giving notice, Sarah."

I nodded.

"You knew?"

"More like felt."

"Been thinking about this a lot. I need to set down what I'm carrying, don't see any other way to do that."

"Understood."

"Brag's good to step up, you want. And what I said before, about talking . . ."

"What'll you do?"

"Nothing right now. Give it time, I think. Sorry to let you down, Sarah."

"You haven't."

"You need two weeks?"

"I don't personally, but it would give others the chance to get used to the idea."

"That would be the twelfth, then."

"Twelfth it is. Headed home?"

"One brief stop before, then yeah."

The stop was at his girlfriend's, to tell Marty the news. As he pulled back into traffic, a pickup shot by and swerved to go around a passenger car, slamming it to the curb before racing on. KC took pursuit, siren wailing. Less than a mile outside town, the pickup pulled over. KC got out, approached, and was shot in the head. From that day he was never again able to take basic care of himself, or to speak. He was twenty-two years old.

22.

When they came, I had on my sweatshirt that read I WAS NEVER HERE, the one Sid gave me, Brag and Special Agent Tyrell Martin at the door, a state trooper behind. Brag apologized, Martin was silent and without affect, the trooper met my eyes once and shook his head. They held me for 48 hours, but we all knew they had no accountable evidence.

They knew. I knew.

As I mentioned back at the first, I didn't do all those things they say I did, but from that moment, stories sprang up, every kind of rumor, shaggy-dog story, tall tale and flight of fancy imaginable. About my past, about Cal, our relationship, his suicide, the murder. Many persist. They rumble off in the distance like thunder.

Why didn't I follow what had always been my standard fallback and move on, away from Farr, from the stories, memories, shunnings, surreptitious glances? It wasn't a conscious decision. I seem to have stopped making those, though I do think at some level I'd reached the conclusion that tucking all under arm and walking away rarely makes you lighter; that instead, step by step, it weighs you down. History has its teeth in you, regardless.

With time, as I went on stubbornly living here, being here, going about what little business I have left, the stares and whispery conversations diminished. The community never brought itself to reembrace me, but I was first tolerated then treated politely and, truthfully, nowadays I feel more alone in the company of others than when by myself.

Not that I'm too terribly often so. Once or twice a week Sid comes over, I cook a meal for us, and afterward we sit together outside, talking some but mostly silent, the sound of so much that was here before us—wind in the trees, cicadas, birdsong—infinitely comforting. Monday and Thursday I cook for residents at Sunny Slope, Saturday for the veterans home two towns over. Some days I get in the pickup and drive, far out into the country and away, but I always come back.

And I visit KC. That's silent too, of course, save for the facility's ever-present ambient noise. Phones ring, carts clatter by, televisions, staff and visitors speak in the hallway as they pass. Weeping, sometimes, and arguments, but there's laughter as well. Most visits, I read to him. We've got through two novels by Dumas and started in on Dickens. Story is what KC and I want, movement, pattern, form. We've no desire nor taste for interiority. There's a surfeit of that already—in the two of us, and in this room.

So here I am, home from Sunny Slope and filling up the last pages of my notebook, not the one we started with way back when I was seven, but one just like it. I had to search long and hard to find one. Can't imagine that I have, or will ever have, any more to say. We're all percipient witnesses to our own lives, aren't we? We look on, watch them happen.

Many's the night I take out Cal's notebook and reread words I know by rote—by heart, as we used to say back home. Words worn into my own life like ruts in old country roads.

The world goes on out there. Interestingly enough, it does fine without you. And: *A voyage around my room, with its two chairs, table, bookshelves, narrow bed, would take four minutes, or forever.*

It does feel like forever, doesn't it? But it's only a moment. It's all only a moment.

Cal's final entry: *I realized this morning that it no longer seems important to go on with this. Whatever I believed this would accomplish has either taken place or failed. I suppose it will be some time before I know, if ever I do.*

Of course we never do.

Moments ago I asked Sid if he will read what I've written here.

"In what capacity?" he said.

"Friend."

He holds out his hand as I inscribe this final period.